*E*mily nudged Sapphire into a trot. He obliged immediately, sliding into the smoothest trot she'd ever experienced. He moved like silk, his gait effortless and powerful.

She sighed with delight as she sank deeper into the saddle, feeling each step he took, listening to the sounds of his hooves as they thudded softly into the grass. His muscles rippled under his coat, and sun reflected off him, making him glisten. The sun beat down on her arms, and she could practically smell it heating up the earth, filling her with light.

A bird flew in front of Sapphire, and he jerked his head up in surprise, jarring her. But she patted his neck, and he settled right down, giving her time to look around at the woods and fields surrounding them as far as she could see.

Lush green, the smell of wetness and spring, no one telling either of them what to do.

She lifted her arms toward the sky and raised her face to the warm sun. "I'm free!" she shouted to the world. "Free!"

Read all the books in the
RUNNING HORSE RIDGE series

HEATHER BROOKS

Running Horse Ridge

1

Sapphire: New Horizons

HarperTrophy®
An Imprint of HarperCollins*Publishers*

Running Horse Ridge #1: Sapphire: New Horizons
Copyright © 2009 by HarperCollins Publishers
All rights reserved. Printed in the United States of America.
No part of this book may be used or reproduced in any manner whatsoever
without written permission except in the case of brief quotations embod-
ied in critical articles and reviews. For information address HarperCollins
Children's Books, a division of HarperCollins Publishers, 1350 Avenue of
the Americas, New York, NY 10019.
www.harpercollinschildrens.com

Library of Congress Cataloging in Publication Data
Brooks, Heather.
 Sapphire: New horizons / Heather Brooks. — 1st ed.
 Summary: Emily Summers travels to Running Horse Ridge, the horse ranch and rescue center
owned by her father's family, and befriends a mischievous black stallion called Sapphire.
 ISBN 978-0-06-142980-4 (pbk.)
 [1. Horses—Fiction. 2. Horsemanship—Fiction. 3. Animal sanctuaries—Fiction.] I. Title.
PZ7.B7943Ne 2009   2008010082
[Fic]—dc22   CIP
                                                                                AC

Typography by Amy Ryan
❖
First Edition

Sapphire: New Horizons

$\mathcal{E}$mily Summers's dad slammed on his brakes and sent her chocolate milk shake spraying all over her favorite pair of jeans. "Dad!"

"Would you rather I hit a horse?" he said, nodding toward the road.

Emily snapped her gaze off her messy jeans just in time to see a gorgeous dark horse skid to a stop in front of the car, his ears back and his teeth bared, as if to challenge the car to a one-on-one battle. He had a glossy black coat and a white blaze down the middle of his face. "He looks like Rhapsody!"

Rhapsody was the horse Emily leased back home in New Jersey. He was the best dressage horse in the barn, and everyone was predicting that he and Emily would be the stars of the Norfolk Open this weekend. Then Emily's grandfather had died suddenly, forcing this trip all the way out to Oregon for his funeral. She'd never met her grandfather, barely even heard of him, and she'd been really upset at first to find out she'd have to miss the show.

Emily had almost asked her dad if he would mind going alone and let her stay with a friend so she could ride Rhapsody. But when her dad had said how much he wanted her with him at the funeral and reminded her that they'd be staying at the horse sanctuary his family had been running for almost seventy-five years, she knew she had to make this trip.

Emily's dad, Scott Summers, hadn't been back to his family farm since Emily's mom had died when Emily was two. He had never talked much about his past, and Emily was curious if he felt weird going home under such sad circumstances after being away for so long. But the few times she'd started to ask him, he'd changed the subject.

Which was okay. She wasn't really sure she wanted to know. It was unsettling to think about her dad being upset. But ever since they'd gotten off the plane, he'd been fiddling with his watch and messing with the dials on the radio constantly. She could tell he was stressed, and it had been making her nervous . . . until the big black horse had jumped in front of their car.

Emily threw open the passenger door and leaped out onto the dirt road, her white tennies sinking into the mud with a squish. It felt like her feet were getting sucked into the mushy ground, like some swamp monster had grabbed her and was going to pull her into the black ooze seeping up around her shoes.

Then the horse snorted, and she forgot about her feet. "Hey, beautiful. Whatchya doing running around out here?"

One ear flicked forward and the horse lifted his head, looking at her with dark, shiny eyes. He was streaked with sweat, dozens of tiny scratches on his chest were bleeding, and his leather halter was muddy. His nostrils flared as he sucked in a noisy breath, scenting Emily to identify her as friend or foe. He was well muscled and well fed, his body rounded out and shiny. His black mane flopped in all directions, and his thick forelock hung on his forehead. His coat was so black that he reminded her of the darkest night.

"Now, Emily, be careful. You don't know this horse," her dad warned as he opened his door and climbed out.

She ignored him and took a step toward the horse, sucking her foot out of the mud with a sloppy slurp. She held her hand out to him as she eased forward. "I bet you escaped from somewhere, didn't you?" she crooned. "You're too pretty to be allowed to run out in front of cars."

The horse's other ear went forward, and he watched Emily intently as she approached.

She felt a wave of homesickness. This horse reminded her so much of Rhapsody, with his shiny black coat and beautiful brown eyes. She was sure that Jenny Smith was going to find a way to ride Rhapsody in the Norfolk Open. It wouldn't be Rhapsody's fault if he had to be ridden by Jenny, but the thought made Emily's stomach clench. Rhapsody was owned by Alice Jenkins, and though Alice always said that if Rhapsody were sold to anybody it would Emily, there was always the chance Jenny would be able to talk Alice into selling Rhapsody to *her* instead. Emily's dad had promised to ask Alice about buying Rhapsody when they got back home because Alice had been hinting lately she might be ready to sell him. If Jenny got him first . . .

The stray horse lowered his head to let her pat him, snuffling softly against her belly. She grinned at her dad and kissed the horse's muddy forehead. "He loves me."

She caught a faint whiff of pine shavings and knew he'd recently been lying in his stall. She pressed her face to his cheek, inhaling the fresh scent she loved, rubbing her skin against his velvet soft hair.

Her dad chuckled. "Actually, he's licking the milk shake off your pants."

Emily looked down and started laughing at the horse using his upper lip to scrape the ice cream off her jeans. "He likes chocolate!"

"Please grab his halter," said a girl's voice.

At the softly spoken request, Emily glanced over her right shoulder to see a girl about her age sitting on a dappled gray mare. She had apparently just ridden up the road behind the car. The girl was wearing leather chaps, an old T-shirt, and a riding helmet, and her horse was breathing hard, her neck streaked with sweat. "His halter," the girl repeated softly, so as not to scare the black horse. "Grab it so he doesn't run away again."

"Right." Emily wrapped her hand around the horse's halter. "Do you have a lead shank?"

The girl lifted a coiled length of leather from the front of her saddle and held it out to Emily's dad. "Will you take this to her? I don't want to get too close or he'll take off again."

Emily's dad took the lead shank and walked over to

Emily, who quietly snapped it onto the horse's halter. The black horse immediately jerked his head up, flattened his ears back, and bared his teeth again.

Emily's dad tried to pull her back. "Watch out, hon—"

"Give me a break, Dad." She tugged on the lead shank. "Hey, beautiful, you're making a scene. That nasty face isn't flattering, and we both know you don't mean it anyway, you big toughie."

The horse glared at Emily and pretended to bite her shoulder. When she didn't shriek and run away, he sighed and dropped his head to lick more milk shake off Emily's jeans instead.

She laughed. "See? I knew he was a faker." She patted his cheek. "Let's go."

She stepped around her dad and led the horse over to the girl. "What's his name?"

"Pain in the Butt."

Emily frowned as the girl took the lead shank from her. "What's his real name?"

"Sapphire. He doesn't deserve it, though. He's a total nightmare." The girl clucked and turned her mount into the fields beside the road. Sapphire pranced along beside them, swishing his tail. "Thanks for your help. I've been chasing him for almost an hour. He drives me insane sometimes."

"No problem. He's really a pretty horse—"

Emily didn't get a chance to finish. As she spoke, the girl kicked her mare into a canter and took off. Then both horses extended into a gallop, and Emily could feel the thunder of their hooves rippling in her body as they pounded across the long field. They arched their necks, ears tipped back against the wind.

Emily stood and watched until they disappeared over a hill, tiny specks in the distance, her belly tightening with envy. "Did you see how fast she went? That was awesome."

She spent all her time training with Rhapsody in a dressage ring, working on the little details of their performance. She rarely let him hack around when she was riding him, and she'd never even dreamed of galloping over a field with him. It looked . . . exhilarating. To feel the wind whipping against her face . . . She couldn't imagine.

Of course, Rhapsody was too valuable to let gallop like that, but still. To do it once . . . on another horse . . . No one at her barn would have to know. "You . . . um . . . think Aunt Debby might let me ride one of her horses? Across the fields?" Emily could almost hear her dressage coach, Les Martin, lecturing her against the bad habits a dressage rider might develop gallivanting outside the ring, and she felt guilty even asking.

When her dad didn't answer, she looked back to see him gazing across the countryside with the oddest look on his face. Like he was sad and happy at the same time, almost as if he were afraid.

Emily shifted, not sure what to say. She'd never seen her dad look scared, and she didn't like it. She swallowed nervously. "Dad? Are you all right?"

He glanced down at her, then smiled and slung his arm over her shoulder, hugging her against his side, immediately making her feel better. "Yes," he said. "I think you'll be able to ride one of Aunt Debby's horses across the fields. These fields, in fact."

She stared at him in surprise. "These fields? These are your fields? *All* these fields?" She looked back out at the landscape stretching before them with renewed interest. There was lush green grass as far as she could see, with clusters of tall pine trees and bushes. The fields were mostly flat, with a few hills rolling in the distance. Not a single building. Not a single car. Just the bright green of fields, every horse's ultimate fantasy.

The grass smelled fresh, and the air smelled so clean and pure. It was incredible. Like you could ride for days and days and days and never run into anyone. Just total freedom and space. So much space. She felt like she could yell until her throat hurt, and no one except her dad would hear her or tell her to be quiet. Nothing like New Jersey, with all its people and cars and buildings and craziness.

The vastness of the land and all the space made her feel small, but also called to her, made her feel like it would lend her its power if she wanted it. She took a deep breath, inhaling nothing but nature and freshness. No exhaust. No food. No sounds except birds and the rustle of the wind through the grasses. No cars. No one yelling. Just total, unspoiled nature.

This was where horses came from. This was where horses were meant to live. It just felt . . . right. "I'm in horse country now, aren't I?" She didn't even need to ask. She could sense it in the air.

He ruffled her hair. "Yep. And if those horses came from our farm that might have been your cousin Alison you just met, too. She'd be fourteen now, a year older than you."

Emily squeaked, unable to contain her excitement. "No way! We're that close to the farm?"

"We're still about five miles away by road—"

Emily gawked at him, unable to believe what he was telling her. Her stuffy, business-suit-wearing dad had grown up in this horse utopia and he'd never bragged about it? "You have *five miles* of fields? How could you not have told me about this place? How could you not have brought me here before?"

His smile faded, and he touched her hair. "It's a long story, Em, but we're here now, right?"

She felt her throat tighten at the sad look on his face and decided to change the subject so he'd smile again. "How many horses live there, exactly?"

A twinkle crept into her dad's eyes, making her sigh with relief. "I don't know how many there are now," he said. "But I think there are around fifty stalls—"

"Fifty? Let's go!" Emily twisted out of her dad's grasp, raced around the car, and flung herself into the passenger seat, not even bothering to knock the mud off her shoes before she slammed the door shut. "Come on!"

Her dad chuckled and slid onto the driver's seat. "Now, remember, this place isn't like the barn at home; these horses aren't top of the line like Rhapsody. And Aunt Debby's not like your riding coach, either. She's . . . harder than Les." He started the engine. "This is a different world out here."

"Horses are horses," Emily murmured, leaning forward as her dad started driving again, trying to catch a glimpse of Sapphire racing across the field. "Of course there's no horse like Rhapsody, but all horses can't be that different. And this place . . . It's special."

He shot her a sideways glance. "Running Horse Ridge *is* special, but it's not even close to your barn back home. Not even close."

Something in his tone caught her attention, and she glanced at him. "What do you mean?"

He hesitated, then patted her leg. "You'll see."

What exactly would she see?

Her dad turned on his left blinker, and she noticed a wooden sign strung across the dirt road. It was weathered, gray, and hanging at an angle. The painted letters were so faded that at first she couldn't read them. But after looking more closely, she worked out what it said: RUNNING HORSE RIDGE.

Emily sat up, her breath caught in her throat, as her dad turned onto the long driveway. *They were here.*

*E*mily clutched the locket with the picture of Rhapsody in her fist as the car bumped over a huge rut and its bottom scraped across the ground, her heart racing with excitement. A horse farm with fifty horses? She couldn't *wait*.

Then they rounded a corner and she frowned. "This is it?" The pasture fence next to the road was half fallen down, strung up with barbed wire, and two saggy gray horses were standing by the road, watching them with total boredom, occasionally flicking their matted tails to get rid of pesky flies. One of them had sores all over its back, covered in some white ointment that was just nasty looking. They looked so sad, she wanted to jump out of the car and run over and hug them. "What's wrong with them? They look awful." *Nothing like Sapphire.*

Or Rhapsody, who loved to run around his green pasture with white fences, tail held high, and his coat reflecting the sun.

Her dad shot her a look. "Remember, this is a horse sanctuary. Some of the horses that arrive here are in pretty bad shape. Debby nurses them back to health or trains them out of behavior problems so they can go on to live a good life at a new home."

"Those poor horses." Her breath left a white fog on the window as she leaned her forehead against the glass. "What about Sapphire? He looked okay."

"He's probably ready to be sold, then."

Emily pressed her lips together against the sudden swell of sadness at the thought of Sapphire being sold. "Really? You think?"

Her dad gave her a surprised look. "Why do you sound upset? You don't even know Sapphire."

"I know, but—" She frowned, realizing her dad was right. She already had Rhapsody, so Sapphire shouldn't matter. Rhapsody had never licked chocolate off her before. Rhapsody ate only grain and top-quality alfalfa hay, and he refused to drink his water unless it was changed three times a day, as was fitting for a horse of his caliber. That's why she loved him. Because he was *perfect*.

Sapphire was . . . well . . . She giggled. He was funny. It was too cute when he'd licked the ice cream off her. And he was beautiful, every bit as beautiful as Rhapsody . . . but different, too. A troublemaker, she'd bet. She just knew he'd be so much fun to ride, because he had a zest for life that . . . well . . . wasn't part of her disciplined existence with Rhapsody and her dressage training. Not that she minded always working hard and taking riding seriously, because she didn't, but something about Sapphire and the sparkle in his eyes called to her. Made her want to be different, even if it was just for a few minutes, just for long enough to take one ride through the fields with him.

Her dad said, "Share the joke?"

"Nothing." She sat up and looked ahead, searching for the barn or the house, but all she saw were pine trees. "So, is the house huge?"

"See for yourself." Emily's dad turned a corner, and Emily sucked in her breath. It was gigantic and sprawling, twenty times the size of their house in New Jersey, and it looked like it had once been gorgeous, but now . . . yikes. It might have been white originally, but there was no way to tell because most of the paint had peeled off. There was some wood propping up one end of the porch, and half the windows didn't even have screens. Really tall fir trees loomed over the house, which was sort of neat, and she liked the huge windows, but . . . "It's . . . um . . . falling down." Their house in New Jersey was brand-new, in a community of identical houses with perfect yards and flawless paint. "It has personality, I guess."

"Don't worry about it falling down. It'll last another two hundred years at least." Her dad tooted the horn and stopped the car as a swayback gray horse wandered in front of them. He was so old he was almost white, but there was a defiance in his eyes that made him look much younger. He paused to give the car a long look, as if ordering them not to run him over. Her dad grinned and leaned on the steering wheel to watch the horse. "That's Max. He was Pa's best friend, and he gets the run of the farm. Goes wherever he wants. I'd forgotten about him."

"Seriously? He wanders around?" Emily felt a flicker of excitement as she watched Max mosey around behind the house. "That's so cool."

The front door of the house swung open, the screen door banging back into the frame with a crash. Emily jerked her gaze up as a woman wearing jeans, a faded red T-shirt, and paddock boots came out on the porch, waving. "Scott! Welcome!"

Her dad tensed, and for a long moment, he didn't respond. He simply stared at the woman as if he'd never seen her before.

Emily shot him a wary look. "Dad? Aren't you going to answer her?"

"Yeah." He took a breath, and a slow smile finally curved over his face. "That's your aunt Debby. I can't believe how long it's been." He opened his door and stood up. "Deb. It's been forever."

There was a slight hesitation, and then her dad hugged his sister hard, as if they both had missed each other so much.

"I'm so sorry about Pa," her dad said. "I wish I'd been here for him."

Aunt Debby hugged him tighter, and Emily felt a little awkward that they were both so sad about their dad, and she'd never met him. Emily never thought of her dad as missing anyone, let alone his family out here, whom he'd barely talked about. She certainly had never thought much about his having a dad, or any family besides herself. She wasn't sure how she felt about sharing him, now that she saw him hugging his sister.

Emily stepped out of the car. The air was fresh and damp, and it felt so clean when she breathed it into her lungs. She had just shut the car door when her dad and Aunt Debby turned to face her.

Aunt Debby had brown hair pulled back in a tight ponytail; she had little laugh lines around her eyes and mouth. She wasn't wearing any makeup. Her eyes were dark brown, and her eyebrows were a little bit frownish.

Then she smiled, and her eyes lit up. "Emily. It's so wonderful to meet you."

"Yeah, you too—" Emily grunted as Aunt Debby threw her arms around her and squashed her in a giant hug. At first Emily froze, then lightly hugged her back, not quite sure what to do.

Aunt Debby pulled away and patted her cheek. "You look just like your mom. Same nose."

Emily's eyebrows shot up at the unexpected reference, touching her fingers to her nose. She didn't remember anything about her mom. She'd peeked every once in a while at her dad's wedding album, but that was more to laugh at her dad's goofy moustache than to look at her mom. She'd never met anyone before who knew her mom, and it felt a little weird. The whole place was feeling a little uncomfortable, actually, with her dad being sad and stressed out, the place being a little more run-down than she expected, and being hugged by family that she didn't know. She shifted, just wanting to go see the horses, where she'd feel comfortable again, to recapture the moment she'd had by the side of the road when she felt so connected to this place where horses belonged. Maybe she could find Sapphire again and let him lick more chocolate off her jeans. "So, um, where's the barn?"

Aunt Debby laughed, a soul deep sound that reverberated in her chest, a sound so contagious it almost made Emily want to laugh out loud with her. Her dad did. "Of course you'd want to see the barn. Scott told me how you're horse crazy." She pointed to her right. "Behind the house and off that way. Your cousins should be around there somewhere. Have fun!"

"Um, okay, thanks." She glanced at her dad. "Okay if I check it out?"

He nodded. "Just for a few minutes, then come back and unpack."

"Sure." She whirled around and broke into a jog, her tennies crunching on the gravel driveway as she rounded the corner, caught the first sight of the barn, and then stopped right where she was.

Like the rest of the farm, the barn was gray and old. Not only were there no polished mahogany doors with brass fixtures, but the doors that were there were nailed together with plywood to keep them from falling apart. But the barn was huge, with a pointed roof that clearly held a hayloft. It reminded her of a barn from the olden days, a true barn, unlike her dressage barn in New Jersey. With its wrought iron chandeliers, glistening paint, and fancy windows, it felt more like a mansion. But this . . . This was a barn in the truest sense of the word.

A big horse van was sitting next to it, and RUNNING HORSE RIDGE was painted on the side in dark green letters that were the same color as the pine trees looming high above the barn. There were paddocks on either side, where horses were turned out, grazing on the grass that was a deeper, more brilliant shade of green than anything Emily had ever seen. It was thick and lush, practically bursting with moisture and life.

The horse nearest her was a dark bay, almost black, with a white face. He snorted once and his tailed swished to clear off invisible bugs, and she felt her heart squeeze as she caught the scent of fresh shavings and hay then drank in the sounds of the horses snuffling for grass. *This was home.*

Her stomach settled and she knew she'd be okay as long as she had the horses. She thought of Sapphire somewhere in that barn, thought of his beautiful face and warm brown eyes, and started walking toward the barn again.

She was running by the time she reached the doors.

Emily ducked inside the barn, taking a moment to let her eyes adjust to the dim light. She inhaled deeply, basking in the scent of horses, of pine shavings, of fresh hay, and felt her insides relax even more. This was her world. Maybe it wasn't as fancy as her barn back home, but it was still where she belonged.

There were stalls along both walls, and she could

see several aisles of more stalls off to the sides. There were no bars on the stall doors, and some of the horses' heads were hanging out; others she couldn't see, and she assumed they were back inside.

The floor was cement and cracked, but it was swept. The barn smelled like lemon and pine, and she knew that someone had just cleaned. The wood, like the rest of the place, looked weathered. But it didn't seem neglected. It felt lived in and comfortable, like it would be okay if the horses wanted to be themselves and kick up some dirt or chew on the door.

Emily wandered over to a liver chestnut with his head hanging out and peeked into his stall. The shavings were fresh, the water was clean, and the horse was brushed. Yeah, the stall door was half chewed and the wall was peppered with divots from a horse kicking it, but it was clean. No automatic watering system that she could see, but it was a good place, she could tell.

She started humming to herself as she strolled down the aisle, peeking in at the stalls, looking for Sapphire. Many of the stalls were empty, and three of the horses tried to bite her as she walked past, making her giggle. "You're not as scary as you think you are," she told a gray horse with his teeth bared. The moment she spoke, he let his lip go back down, and his ears cocked forward to listen to her. "See? I knew it."

One horse she passed had a big shaved patch on his hip and a huge scar, and another had a bandage totally covering his right eye. Most were dozing, one hind leg cocked with their heads hanging contentedly in sleep. There were open doors on the far side of the stalls, leading to the pasture. She could see a few horses out there, and could practically touch the happiness in the air.

Some looked fat and well fed, and others . . . not so much. On one horse in a stall, she could even see his ribs, and she gave him a few moments of scratching time while he munched on the big pile of hay. He might be thin, but he was getting food now. She realized that it was cool, actually, what Aunt Debby did. Saving horses that needed help. She'd never thought about it before, but there was something about seeing those needy horses in clean stalls that just made her feel good.

She heard the murmur of voices as she passed the tack room and peeked inside to check it out. There were no brass saddle racks and glistening white saddle pads, but the saddles were clean and the red saddle racks wouldn't look so bad if the paint wasn't half peeled off. There were a couple kids in there, cleaning tack, and she grinned, thinking about the hours she spent in the tack room at her own barn, hanging out. Not so different here.

She reached the end of the aisle and stepped outside past a heavy door that had been propped open with a dinged-up, gray wheelbarrow loaded with three big bags of shavings.

She heard the thud of hooves and glanced to her right. A riding arena! Brightly colored jumps were set up, and the girl she'd met out on the road was racing over them on the dapple gray she'd been riding in the field.

But Sapphire was nowhere to be seen. Was someone taking care of his cuts? She headed over to the ring to ask the girl.

Emily reached the ring and leaned on the fence, waiting for the girl to take a break so she could ask about Sapphire. The girl's hair was flying, her elbows were sticking out and flailing, her heels were up, and she was shouting encouragement to the horse as they sprang over a red and white striped jump that looked huge. At least three feet high. The girl was wild and all over the place and clearly didn't care one bit about her form, but her horse seemed to be doing things right, so maybe she was a good rider even if she didn't *look* like one.

Emily spent *hours* working on her form with Rhapsody. They could have one lesson just on walking because the little details were that important.

This girl obviously didn't bother with the details.

Dirt sprayed up from the horse's hooves as he flew around a corner and sprang over a jump. The horse was fit and she was flying over the huge jumps with no problem. It actually looked sort of fun, and Emily felt a trickle of jealousy that she wasn't the one riding . . . Not that she was into jumping, of course.

She was all about dressage . . . She did another check of the ring. No dressage letters on the sides, even as a backup for when they took the jumps out of the ring.

There had to be a dressage ring around somewhere, didn't there?

She saw a boy about ten years old squatting next to a bucket. One of her cousins? She walked over to him. "Hi. Is there a dressage ring here?"

He looked up at her, his bright red hair a total mess and his cheeks sunburned. "You're my cousin Emily?"

She nodded. "What's your name?" Her dad had mentioned a boy, but she'd been too busy fantasizing about the horses to pay attention.

"Kyle." He pulled a squirt gun out of the bucket

and popped the plug in and started pumping the chamber. "Nice clothes."

She looked down at her new jeans and top and her white tennis shoes that were now muddy. "Thanks. I got them for the trip here— Hey!"

She was hit in the chest with a flood of water, and then he cackled with laughter and sprinted around the corner of the barn before she could stop him. "You little jerk!"

"He's always like that. Ignore him."

Emily looked up to see the girl on the horse had reined in to a walk and was cruising along the rail, watching her. She was wearing no makeup and there was dirt on her cheek, but Emily thought she was beautiful. She had a little nose, perfect mouth, and gorgeous green eyes.

Emily suddenly felt a little plain. And wet.

"I'm Alison. You're Emily?"

Emily squeezed out her shirt and water droplets landed in the dirt. "Yeah. Do you, um, have a dressage ring around here?"

"Dressage?" Alison snorted as her horse cruised past, still breathing heavily. "No way. We're all about hunter/jumper here."

Emily stiffened. "You say it like dressage is a bad thing."

"It's not bad. It's just boring."

"It's not boring! It's incredibly difficult. It's . . . it's ballet for horses, a classic training program that's, like, two thousand years old. Do you even have any idea how many different things you have to think about when the horse is walking?"

"Yeah, one. How to get him to go faster."

"Faster? That's it?" Emily hooked her arms tighter around the fence rail, starting to get a little upset. She could tell Alison didn't think much of dressage, and it was making her feel like she didn't belong—like because she was a dressage rider, she wouldn't fit in at their barn, wouldn't be good enough to be a part of things here. "Dressage is about so much more than speed. It's beautiful and precise and—"

"Well, we don't do dressage around here," Alison interrupted. "Is that all you do? Mom said you'd be able to help with the horses, but if all you do is dressage, I'm not sure how much you're going to be able to do with them. We rehab the horses and retrain them for hunter/jumper competition."

Emily felt her stomach tighten at the implication that she wouldn't be good enough to ride their horses. "I'm a good rider, actually. Rhapsody and I were the favorites at the Norfolk Open this weekend in the Level

III test—" She stopped at Alison's blank look. "Never mind," she mumbled.

At her barn everyone knew how well she and Rhapsody did together. Every Monday after a show, everyone congratulated her. She didn't have to prove herself, but here . . . It had never even crossed her mind she wouldn't fit in at this barn. Family she didn't know was one thing, but the barn? She lifted her chin. "I'm good enough to ride the horses here. I'll be helpful."

Alison raised an eyebrow and shrugged. "You'll have to take it up with my mom. She's the boss. It would be nice to have help, though, so I hope you're right."

"I'm right. I'll be fine."

"That would be good." Alison gathered up the reins. "I'll see you later, I guess. I'm going to go cool her down with a run through a stream." Alison turned her horse away, trotted over to the gate, and unhooked the latch with her foot.

"Wait!" Emily scrambled off the fence and jogged over to the gate needing more than ever to see Sapphire. He liked her, she knew it, and she needed to be around him, even if it was just long enough for her to give him a hug. "Where's Sapphire? I wanted to visit him."

"Last stall in the south aisle." Alison rode her horse out the gate, then paused to look at Emily. "But be careful. My mom's superprotective of Sapphire. She has high hopes for him." Then she whirled around and took off in a thud of hoofbeats along a grassy path that headed back toward a patch of trees. Dirt sprayed against Emily's legs as Alison took off, releasing the scent of fresh, wet earth into the air.

Emily stared after her, watching with envy as she disappeared in the woods. Not that she wanted to be reckless and crazy like Alison . . . but to be able to ride off by herself like that? Too cool. "This is so different from home," she said.

"Where's home?"

She spun around to see a little girl standing next to her, chewing on a piece of hay. The girl looked about seven and was wearing filthy cutoff jeans and a T-shirt that had mud all over it. "Where's your home?" she asked again.

Emily smiled at the thought of the place where she knew how to fit in. "New Jersey."

"Why is that home?"

"Because that's where my friends are."

"Oh." The girl thought about this for a moment. "Well, I'm Caitlyn. I'll share my friends with you. They're nice."

Emily couldn't help but laugh, and some of her tension

eased. "Well, thanks. I appreciate that."

"My friend Tanya and I are building a fort in the hay barn right now. I came out to get some horse blankets to sit on. Want to come?"

Emily glanced at the barn, toward Sapphire's stall. "I can't right now. I have to go check on a horse."

"Oh . . . " Caitlyn nodded. "You're Emily, then? You're going to live with us now?"

"For a little bit."

"Mommy says she hopes you'll never leave. That you'll stay forever."

"Forever? No. We're just here for the funeral. . . . " Then she frowned. Unless her dad hadn't told her something . . . Was that why he hadn't talked to Alice about buying Rhapsody yet, even though his owner had been dropping hints that she would be willing to sell him?

Granted it was completely awesome to be on a horse farm and all, but this wasn't home. This wasn't her world. She didn't want to *stay* here. There wasn't even a dressage ring!

Not that her dad would do that . . . or would he? What if he got here and realized he'd missed it too much ever to leave again?

"Emily? You need to unpack! Come back to the house." Her dad's voice echoed across the farm.

"Okay, so I'll see you, then." Caitlyn wheeled around and skipped her way into the barn.

"Em!"

"I'll be there in a second!" Not ready to question her dad in case he had answers she didn't want to hear, answers that meant she'd be staying in a world where she didn't quite fit, Emily squeezed out her shirt again from the squirt gun attack then jogged back into the barn to find Sapphire.

Then she stopped, realizing she had no idea which way was south. What kind of information was that? South? In New Jersey, it was "take a left" not "south aisle."

She guessed, turned right, and found him in the last stall. He was snoozing at the back of the stall, his head dangling, his right back foot cocked in rest. He was wearing a cotton sheet with holes in it to absorb his sweat while he cooled down. The sweat sheet was a faded royal blue with light blue trim and white piping and a little too small for him, but he still looked majestic with his broad shoulders and muscled neck. "Sapphire!"

He jerked his head up and swung it around to peer at her, and his chocolate brown eyes were shiny even in the dim light of the barn.

"It's me. Emily!"

His ears went forward, then he let out a soft nicker of greeting that made her grin, and she knew everything would be all right.

4

apphire ambled to the front of his stall as she unlocked the door. By the time she got inside, he was already snuffling her jeans for any leftover ice cream. "Sapphire." She sighed as she wrapped her arms around him and pressed her face to his neck. His coat was so soft, and he smelled like pine shavings and a hint of salty sweat. She rubbed her face against his mane, and the hairs prickled her cheek. She sighed in complete ecstasy. "You were so worth coming across the country for."

He nickered again and started to nibble on the edge of her shirt, so she pulled back and patted his neck. She scratched behind his ears as she lifted the front of the sheet to check his chest, giggling when he wiggled his lip in her hair. Someone had cleaned out the scratches and put cream on them. "You're all good, huh?"

He lowered his beautiful head and snorted against her jeans as she dropped the sheet back down. "Sorry, you already ate all the chocolate." She scratched his neck again, frowning when dried sweat flaked off under her nails. "You need some brushing, don't you, sweetie? Hang on one sec and I'll be back."

She locked him in and scavenged the aisle until she found a well-stocked grooming bucket nearby. She filched a round rubber currycomb and a dandy brush, then slipped back inside, grinning when he shoved his face against her belly. "Hi, beautiful. Didja miss me?"

She unhooked his sweat sheet, tossed it over the door, and began to curry him, being careful around his scratches. She worked the dried sweat out of his shiny coat. He turned his head to watch her, his ears pricked forward as she chattered to him. "So, anyway, I'm here because my granddad died. Did you know him? My dad says he was cool, but I never met him. He was a vet, like my uncle."

Sapphire swished his tail as she started working on his rump, his muscles rippling under his coat. Emily chuckled as she caught his tail. "No lashing my face with the coarse tail hairs, my friend." She started picking shavings out of his tail, grinning as he kept trying to yank his tail free. He finally started walking in circles, forcing her to walk along with him.

Sapphire kept looking back at her, eyes twinkling and ears perked, as if he were laughing at her.

"Just so you know, Rhapsody always stands perfectly still when I work on him," she told him. "But I have to admit, this is far more fun."

He immediately swished his tail so hard it flew out of her hands and nearly jerked her over. She laughed and set her hands on her hips. "You're a troublemaker, aren't you?"

He ducked his head as if he were going to lick her jeans, then pressed his forehead against her hip and gave her a hard shove, knocking her right onto her butt. She grinned up at him as he snuffled her lap for treats, his giant hooves carefully placed next to her feet so he didn't accidentally step on her.

She grinned and scratched behind his ears. "I'll bring you some treats next time. Maybe a pan of brownies? Would that do it?"

"Emily?" There was a disbelieving note in her aunt's voice as she appeared in the doorway.

"Oh, hi." Emily patted Sapphire's neck and scrambled

to her feet. "I was just cleaning him up. He was all sweaty. Hope that's okay?"

Aunt Debby's face looked annoyed. "Actually, it's not. I'm trying hard to improve his behavior around the barn, and he needs to be on cross ties at all times when you're working with him. Encouraging him to knock you down isn't going to help my training."

Emily felt her cheeks heat up. "I'm sorry. I was just trying to be helpful, and it wasn't like he hurt me or anything."

Emily's dad appeared in the doorway. To Emily's surprise, he'd changed out of his brown slacks and polished loafers and was now wearing faded blue jeans and a pair of work boots. She didn't even know he owned faded jeans. He looked like a rugged farmer guy now, instead of the businessman she was used to seeing. Not her dad at all.

"Oh, give her a break, Deb," he said. "How was she to know? I think it's nice that she was cleaning him up without anyone asking."

Aunt Debby frowned, but she nodded. "You're right. Emily, thanks for cleaning him up, but in the future, make sure you use the cross ties, okay? And don't let him knock you down. We're really trying to break him of that habit."

Sapphire set his chin on Emily's shoulder and snorted. Emily reached up to pat his cheek, marveling at how soft his coat was. "No problem. I'll do the cross ties. Can I finish cleaning him up now?" She looked at her dad. "Unpack later?"

He shook his head. "I need to head into town to make some calls because my cell phone doesn't work out here, and I was thinking we could stop at the grocery store and get some things you might like to snack on."

She sighed, totally reading her dad: He wasn't about to leave her behind while he went into town. Probably afraid she'd get into more trouble. "Fine. Can I come back later to finish him?"

"I'll take care of him," Aunt Debby said. "You get settled."

Emily bit her lip as Aunt Debby walked into the stall and hooked Sapphire up to the cross ties, wanting so much to stay with him. "Can I maybe ride Sapphire sometime?"

Her aunt gave her an appraising look as she started to rub down Sapphire, much harder than Emily had been doing, really getting the dirt out in a way Emily hadn't. "Tell you what. I'll give you a lesson in the morning, and we'll see where you are and then make a decision. Sound good?"

"Really? That would be awesome." Emily grinned with excitement. Finally! She was going to get to ride! "What time?"

"Eight."

"Eight?" Emily blinked. Getting up for an eight o'clock lesson while she was on vacation?

"The funeral's at noon."

Oh, right. The funeral. She suddenly felt bad for making a big deal of the time. "Eight's fine."

Aunt Debby nodded. "There's a whiteboard inside the tack room. Check it when you get to the barn. I'll have written down the name of the horse you'll be riding, and you can grab its tack and get ready. Okay?"

"Could I put in a request for Sapphire?"

Aunt Debby smiled. "You can, but it won't make a difference. You're not riding him until I know you've got the skills."

"But—"

Emily's dad took her arm. "Come on, Em. You can prove yourself in the morning. The only decent grocery store's about a half hour away, so we need to get going."

Emily twisted free and ran over to Sapphire, wrapped her arms around his neck, and buried her face in his silky coat. "I'll see you tomorrow, Sapphire." She kissed his nose then spun and ran after her dad, who had already started walking.

Her dad chuckled and clapped his hand on her shoulder as they headed down the aisle. "Looks like Rhapsody may be history, huh? No longer the favorite?"

"What?" Emily cast one last glance over her shoulder at Sapphire, grinning when he tried to push Aunt Debby over. "I have to be able to ride Sapphire before we leave, Dad."

Her dad ruffled her hair. "Aunt Debby's a stickler when it comes to her horses. You're going to have to prove yourself to her."

"I will." She clenched her fists, knowing that it all depended on her lesson tomorrow.

She had to impress Aunt Debby. *She had to.*

*E*mily was giddy with excitement by the time she got to the tack room the next morning for her lesson. She'd gotten up early to polish her paddock boots, even though she never ever polished them, because they were only for hanging out at the barn. And she'd even taken the time to put up her hair under her helmet the way she did for a show, making sure no stray strands were poking out. Aunt Debby would see her and realize that Emily was serious when it came to riding, and she'd have no choice but to let her ride Sapphire.

She practically skipped into the tack room to look at the whiteboard, and saw she was listed to ride a horse named Moondance, with a little note about which stall she was in. The moment Emily saw her name up there, butterflies swarmed her belly. This was it: her moment to prove herself.

Emily found the bridle with Moondance's name, then frowned when she realized her hand was shaking when she went to pick it up. What was wrong with her? She was a good rider and she knew it.

She hooked the bridle over her shoulder and scanned the racks for Moondance's saddle, biting her lower lip at the thought of what would happen if she did a terrible job in the lesson. Aunt Debby, Alison, and everyone else here would never accept her. She already felt like a stranger, even though they were family, and riding was the only way she knew how to fit in. If she failed at that . . .

No. This was ridiculous. Of course she'd be good enough. Everything would be *fine*.

She tucked Moondance's saddle against her hip, grabbed a fully stocked brush box, and headed out. After detouring by Sapphire's stall to give him a few treats and some love, she traipsed down to Moondance's stall and hoisted her saddle onto its wooden bar.

Emily opened the door and saw a plain gray mare snoozing in the corner. "Good morning. I'm Emily."

Moondance lifted her head to inspect Emily, and

then dropped her head back down and went back to sleep. Emily grinned, suddenly feeling at ease again as she stepped into Moondance's stall. This was Emily's world, and she was in control. "Yeah, I have mornings like that, too, when I just want to stay in bed. But we'll have fun, trust me."

Moondance didn't look impressed as Emily dropped the brush box in the corner then pulled out a curry-comb and started to rub the mare down. Emily frowned at the manure stains on Moondance's hips from sleeping in her stall. After currying the same spot for about ten minutes, Emily finally gave up. "You, my beautiful, need a bath. Gray horses are impossible to keep clean." She affectionately tweaked Moondance's ear. "Especially when they roll in manure during the night."

Moondance lifted her upper lip at Emily, making Emily laugh. "Yeah, I can see you feel really bad about it, too."

Emily recalled when Jenny Smith at her barn had pitched a fit when she'd arrived in the morning of a show last summer and the horse she'd been riding had laid down during the night. Jenny had been so mad at her mount sporting yellow stains, and she'd had to give her a bath again at four in the morning after she was already dressed in her polished boots and sparkling clean, beige jodhpurs.

That was the first time Jenny had started eyeing Rhapsody, because he'd come out of his stall just as clean and shiny as he'd been when Emily had put him in the night before, with his beautiful black coat. And then when Emily had beaten Jenny that day . . . the war had begun.

She frowned as she grabbed a hoof pick and slid her hand down Moondance's leg, giving a small tug when she reached her fetlock and leaning into the horse with her shoulder. Moondance obediently shifted her weight and let Emily pick up her foot.

As she used the metal pick to flick mud and rocks out of Moondance's hoof, being careful not to hit the tender frog in the middle of the foot, she thought about the Norfolk Open coming up. Would Jenny get to ride Rhapsody? Maybe Emily should call one of her friends and find out. . . .

As she picked out the rest of Moondance's feet, she tried to decide whether she'd want to know about Jenny or not, her belly tightening the more she thought about it. Moondance snorted and gave her a nudge, and Emily grinned. "You think I should stop obsessing, huh?"

The horse had a point. She was about to get her first jumping lesson *ever*. That was too cool for words. Jenny wasn't getting a jumping lesson today, was she?

Emily hummed to herself, grabbed the bridle, and put it on.

Well, tried.

The moment she got the bit near Moondance's teeth, the mare lifted her head and pointed her nose to the ceiling, completely out of Emily's reach. When Emily dropped the bridle, Moondance lowered her head back down as if nothing was wrong.

"Okay, so you like to be difficult, is that it?" Emily took the bridle and wrapped her arm around Moondance's nose to hold her down. Then she used her left hand to guide the bit into Moondance's mouth . . . then Moondance yanked her head right out of Emily's grasp and pointed her nose to the ceiling again.

Emily growled with frustration and let her hands drop as she eyed the underside of Moondance's throat, which was all she could see of the horse's head from this angle. "Okay, so you want war, is that it?" She set her hands on her hips and chewed her lower lip as she realized what was going on. "This was a test from Aunt Debby, wasn't it?"

Moondance shook her head and wandered to the back of the stall to take a nap.

"You think I'm giving up? No way."

Emily peeked out into the aisle, found a big plastic tub for soaking hay in water for horses with asthma who couldn't handle the hay dust. It was empty, at least two feet high, and perfect. She grinned, dragged it into Moondance's stall, and turned it upside down in front of her. The mare dropped her head to sniff it while Emily gathered the bridle for the third time and then climbed on top of the tub so she towered above Moondance's back.

"Now, let's try this again, shall we?"

She put her right arm under and then around Moondance's nose to hold the bridle in place, and set the bit in front of her teeth. As before, Moondance lifted her head straight toward the ceiling, but this time Emily followed her with her arms, stuck her finger in the corner of Moondance's mouth to get her to open her teeth, then slipped the bit right inside. She grinned as she pulled the bridle over each ear. "See? That wasn't so bad."

Once the bridle was secure over her ears, Moondance sighed and dropped her head back down in defeat. Emily patted her neck and hopped off the tub to buckle the throatlatch and the noseband. "Why do I bet you'd do this every single time I tried to ride you?"

Moondance snorted and stomped her back foot, and Emily grinned. "Yeah, that's what I thought."

She tossed the tub back in the aisle, put the saddle on, and tightened the girth, then headed out to the ring, her heart beating with excitement. She couldn't wait for Aunt Debby to admit she was a great rider, good enough to ride Sapphire.

This was going to be excellent.

It took five minutes of riding before Emily started getting used to the hunt saddle. It felt really bulky in comparison to the dressage saddle, and she kept wanting to take the knee pads out . . . except there weren't any that she could see. It just *felt* like they were there. She checked three times, so she knew.

Moondance was bigger than Rhapsody, so it felt weird to be on a horse with such a long stride. Plus, she liked to walk with her head way up high, unlike Rhapsody, who was so good about dropping his head and getting on the bit, which basically meant that his nose was in a straight line toward the ground and his butt was tucked under him in proper dressage form.

Moondance kept lifting her head high, above Emily's hands, so it was difficult to feel like Emily had good contact with her mouth, and the mare didn't like to bend her body with the turns the way Rhapsody did.

Emily clenched her jaw as she went through all the

reminders Les gave her when she was riding Rhapsody, trying to get Moondance to walk properly, but she couldn't get the mare to drop her head. Emily felt like pulling her hair out. Why was it this hard to do what she did all the time?

She finally closed her eyes and focused on riding by feel, altering pressure with her calves to keep Moondance moving forward briskly while ever so gently playing with the reins to get Moondance to listen to them. She sank her fanny deep into the saddle so she could feel every step, every muscle in Moondance shift as she walked. Finally, she felt Moondance begin to relax and her head dropped down so she was on the bit. Not as nicely as Rhapsody did it, but pretty darn good.

She opened her eyes and grinned, completely impressed with herself. Aunt Debby would have to know how hard it was to get Moondance in a frame, and she'd go crazy over what Emily had done.

Emily was walking Moondance around the ring in a collected, balanced, and really excellent walk when Aunt Debby showed up. Emily checked her position, made sure her heels were down, and waited for Aunt Debby to compliment her.

"Your stirrups are too long. You need them shorter for jumping."

Emily blinked. "What?" Hadn't she noticed the walk?

"Jumping. That's what we do." Aunt Debby ducked under the rail and stepped in front of Moondance.

Emily hastily reined Moondance to a stop, and the mare's head popped out of frame, losing everything Emily had spent the last twenty minutes working on!

Aunt Debby didn't even seem to notice as she quickly shortened Emily's stirrups until Emily felt like a jockey, then gave Emily's knee a pat and told her to move on. "Are you warmed up?"

Emily shifted in the saddle, trying to get used to the short stirrups. How could she possibly sit deep enough when her feet were jacked up so short? She felt like her knees were in her chest. Of course, they weren't, but her knees *were* bent a lot more than when she was in her dressage saddle. She stood in her stirrups, pressing her heels down to try to get more length. "I've been walking for about twenty minutes—"

"You've been walking all this time?" Aunt Debby sounded a little surprised, and Emily suddenly felt like she'd done something wrong.

"I wasn't supposed to?"

Aunt Debby shook her head. "It's not a big deal. Next time, go ahead and get fully warmed up before

I get here, so we can get right to work." She glanced at her watch. "We only have about forty-five minutes, so get going. Fortunately, Moondance doesn't require much warm-up."

"Um, okay." Emily gathered her reins and nudged Moondance into a trot, nearly popping out of the saddle at the long, rocking stride. Moondance's head was up in the air again, making her gait bumpy. Emily got the rhythm of the trot quickly, though, and started doing a posting trot, rising out of her seat each time Moondance's outside front leg went forward.

She still felt like Moondance wasn't collected, so she did a small circle to try to get the mare to come back to her.

"Emily, just let her go. Stop tugging at the reins."

"But I'm trying to get her on the bit—"

"This isn't dressage, Emily. She doesn't need to drop into a frame right now. Just let her warm up."

"Really?"

"Really. Soften your hands, let her stretch her muscles."

"But isn't that lazy riding? Not to do anything?" Emily loosened the reins a little.

"You should still be working. I just want you not to try to turn Moondance into a dressage horse. Go ahead and canter." Aunt Debby walked into the middle of the ring and started lowering the jumps that Alison had been jumping yesterday.

"Canter already?"

"Already."

"Well, okay." Emily clucked and nudged Moondance into a canter. The mare swished her tail in annoyance, and Emily gave her a harder nudge. She finally cantered, a rough, awkward beat that nearly jarred Emily off the saddle, so unlike Rhapsody's smooth gait that was so comfortable she could sit for hours without even rocking Emily's upper body a tiny bit. Emily sat deep in the saddle and tried to bring Moondance back under her, driving her weight into her haunches and trying to get Moondance balanced so that her gait wasn't as jarring.

"Stop tugging on her," Aunt Debby said. "Let her get loose and warmed up. Get up in a half-seat and let her relax."

"A half-seat? What's that?"

"Lift your butt out of the saddle. Stand in your stirrups the way jockeys do."

"*Oh.*" Emily stood in the saddle and was surprised at how much easier it was to handle Moondance's jarring gait when she wasn't trying to sit deep in the saddle. Interesting. It was actually kind of liberating and fun. She loosened the grip on the reins a little more and clucked to urge Moondance to go a little faster.

The mare's ears flicked back toward Emily as she picked up speed, and Emily grinned at the wind rushing past. It was fun. Liberating. To just ride.

She changed direction by cutting through the middle, dropping to a trot, and then picking up a canter again in the new direction, picking up the correct lead for the new direction, making sure Moondance was leading with her inside front leg to stay balanced.

She was having so much fun cantering that it took several times before she finally heard Aunt Debby tell her to walk. Flushing, she sat back in the saddle and slowed down her mount, grinning as Moondance did a little jig to the side before finally walking. "She likes to go fast."

"I'm training her to compete in jumper classes," Aunt Debby explained. "When she competes, she races against the clock, so she's used to going fast."

"Oh, that's so cool. Can I race against the clock?" That sounded like tons of fun.

"Sure, once you're ready." Aunt Debby pointed her to a jump made of two red and white painted rails propped up in a giant X. The middle was only about a foot high, tiny compared to the jumps Alison had been going over. "Get up in half-seat, trot up to the crossbar, and jump it."

It was time to jump.

6

$\mathcal{E}$mily bit her lip, her heart starting to pound. She'd never jumped anything before, other than trotting over a rail lying on the ground. It had never even occurred to her to jump. "You could put it higher if you want. Like what Alison was jumping."

A faint smile played across Aunt Debby's face. "Why don't we start with the cross rail and then move on?"

"Okay." Emily felt a glimmer of excitement as she gathered up her reins and nudged Moondance into a trot. She looked ahead to the jump, planning out her line of approach. As she turned right toward the jump and straightened Moondance out so the mare wasn't coming at the jump from an angle, Aunt Debby called out more instructions.

"Grab onto Moondance's mane when you get near the jump. It'll help until you get used to the movement."

Grab her mane? Like some inexperienced rider? No way. Emily pressed down her heels, lifted her chin, and moved into half-seat as they approached, setting her hands *on* the mane, but not actually *grabbing* the mane because she was far too good for *that*.

Moondance trotted up to the jump, pricked her ears, and did a little hop with her front legs to go over it.

"Whoa!" Emily lost her balance, almost fell over backward, then crashed face-first into Moondance's mane when they landed on the other side. Moondance landed in a canter, and Emily grabbed her mane to keep from falling off and landing on her head. She wiggled her way back into her saddle, bracing her hands on Moondance's neck to shove herself in place, then she grabbed the reins and eased Moondance back to a trot.

She slipped a sideways glance at Aunt Debby, her face hot with embarrassment. "I'm better than that."

"Emily, it's not a problem. It's a new experience to jump. I'm not worried."

"Oh." Emily felt better. "Okay, then. Again?"

Aunt Debby sat down on one of the bigger jumps.

"Again. Hold the mane this time."

"Yeah, okay." This time, Emily grabbed Moondance's mane just before the mare hopped over the jump, and though Emily got left behind again, it wasn't nearly as bad because she was yanked forward by her grip on the mane.

She grinned at her aunt as Moondance cantered after the jump. "That is *so fun*."

Aunt Debby smiled. "Well, do it again."

This time, as they approached the jump, Emily held tight and kept up with Moondance as the mare flew into the air. They landed, and Emily let out a small whoop of excitement that made Moondance do a little jig. "Did you see that? We were airborne!"

Aunt Debby laughed. "I take it you like jumping?"

"It's awesome! Can I go again?"

"Of course. This time, keep on cantering and jump the vertical that's after the crossbar."

Emily's heart thumped as she inspected the red-and-white-striped bar stretched between the two wooden standards. It was about a foot high and looked extremely impressive. "Just canter it?"

"Yep. Count the strides after you land from the crossbar, including the landing. It should take six steps to reach it, but definitely hold the mane."

"Oh, *yeah.*" Her heart racing now, Emily trotted Moondance toward the crossbar, grabbed the mane, and soared through the air with her. She counted the strides out loud with her aunt as they cantered down the line, holding Moondance straight between her legs. "Land, one, two, three, four, five, six—"

Moondance leaped into the air, and Emily forgot to grab the mane. Her upper body went flying backward, totally left behind, and then she jerked forward when Moondance landed, shooting over the mare's shoulder and crashing to the soft dirt by Moondance's front feet.

Moondance stopped immediately and turned her head to peer at her while Emily rolled to her knees, her heart racing as she caught her breath after the tumble.

Aunt Debby was by her side immediately. "Are you okay?"

"Oh, yeah." Emily grinned, unable to suppress her glee. Jumping was so exhilarating. So freeing! "This is so much fun!"

Her aunt smiled and rapped her knuckles on Emily's helmet. "Well, have a go again, then. I'll give you a leg up."

"Right on." Emily hopped to her feet, brushed off her breeches, and walked over to Moondance. She bent her left knee, lifting her foot off the ground so it was pointing behind her, and Aunt Debby clasped her fingers under Emily's knee.

"On three. One, two, three!" She hoisted Emily up and Emily hopped at the same time, and she flew up and swung her leg over Moondance's back.

She settled in the saddle, gathered her reins, and picked up a trot again.

"This time, hold on to her mane."

"Got it." Emily wrapped her fingers in Moondance's mane as they approached, grinning as she leaped over the crossbar and headed toward the vertical. "Land, one, two, three, four, five, six!" She held tight to her mane as the horse sprang into the air and still got a little left behind, but not nearly as badly because she was gripping the mane so tightly. She glanced at Aunt Debby as they cantered after the jump. "What am I doing wrong? Why am I getting left behind?"

"Nothing, you're doing great. It just takes a while to get used to the movement of jumping. You'll get the feel of it."

"Okay." Emily had new appreciation for the size of the jumps Alison had been going over. They'd been at least three times as big, and Alison hadn't had any problem. How fun would it be to jump that high? She couldn't *wait* until she got that good. "When do I get to jump higher jumps?"

Aunt Debby laughed. "Why don't we master this level first?"

"I don't care if I fall off."

"Well, I do, and you should, too." Her hands went to her hips, and the smile was replaced by a bit of a scowl. "It's important to master the basics before you move on. Otherwise you can end up endangering yourself and the horse. In my barn, I expect you to be responsible with the horses at all times, which means not taking crazy risks like going over jumps you don't have the skills to handle."

Emily winced at the serious tone in her aunt's voice. "Okay," she quickly said. "This height is fine."

"Good. Now do it again."

Emily did it again. And again. And again.

And it never stopped being a thrill when she had that moment in the air before Moondance thudded back to the ground. It was, quite simply, the coolest thing she'd ever done on a horse.

Not that she was going to turn into a jumper, because the discipline of dressage was, of course, her thing, but there was something about jumping that was so unbelievably exhilarating, and she couldn't *wait* until she could go fast and race against the clock.

After about a half hour of jumping, Emily finally figured out the rhythm of the jump and managed to keep up with Moondance most of the time, though she still held on to the mane at takeoff. Each time she thought about letting go, she got left behind again and realized she wasn't ready.

Soon, though. She was so determined to master jumping before she left. She knew her jumping experience wouldn't truly be complete until she got to do it on Sapphire. When Aunt Debby looked at her watch and announced it was time to stop, Emily was so disappointed. "Already?"

Aunt Debby smiled, a real smile that didn't make her brow get all furrowed. "We've been out here for almost an hour."

"Seriously?" Emily glanced at her watch and was amazed to see it was almost nine thirty. "Wow."

"We'll practice more tomorrow."

"On Sapphire?" Emily held her breath as she circled Moondance around Aunt Debby, her reins loose and relaxed to let Moondance cool down.

"I'm sorry, Emily. I know you really like him, but he's a bit difficult, especially over the jumps. He's my special project and you're not ready to ride him yet."

Emily bit her lip. "But soon?"

Aunt Debby started to head toward the gate. "We'll see."

Shoot. That was adult-speak for "never." "Why is he your special project? Alison said you're going to sell him." She trailed along after Aunt Debby, patting Moondance for being such a good girl.

Aunt Debby opened the gate and met Emily's gaze. "That's what we do here, Em. I buy horses with potential that have issues, either training issues or health issues. Then I try to fix them and sell them for a profit. Sapphire was a bargain and he's a beautiful horse, so I'm planning to make a nice profit from him."

Emily bit her lip. "Why don't you keep him?"

"Because it's not how the farm works. We don't keep them."

"But he's special—"

"Emily." Aunt Debby set her hand on Emily's knee, her eyes sympathetic. "Sapphire isn't going to stay, okay? He just isn't. I need to sell him."

"When?"

"When he's ready." Aunt Debby started walking again.

Emily nudged Moondance out the gate so she could

follow her aunt. "When's that? Tomorrow?"

Aunt Debby finally laughed. "Emily, relax. It'll be a few months, okay?"

"Okay." A few months. Plenty of time to convince her aunt not to sell him.

"But you're leaving soon. Why does it matter to you?"

Emily felt her face heat up, a little embarrassed to admit how much she liked Sapphire even though she'd just met him. "I was just asking."

"Mmm." Aunt Debby held up her watch. "We leave in an hour for the funeral. Don't be late."

Ugh. A funeral. She'd so much rather be hanging out at the barn. "Yeah, okay."

Aunt Debby raised her brows. "Don't sound so miserable. It's a good thing to go and honor your Grandfather, even if you didn't get the chance to know him."

Emily tensed. Her dad was the only one who ever cared about her, and it was weird to think that she had other relatives. "Really?"

"Really."

"Did you love him?"

Aunt Debby's face softened. "Of course I did. He was my pa."

"So, how come you don't seem sad? I'd be crying all the time."

"Because this is how life works. Just like the horses come and go from the farm, people come and go in our lives. We enjoy the good moments, and when we're in the bad ones, we just hang on until things get good again."

Emily frowned as she thought about that. "So, you're saying, I should just enjoy Sapphire while he's here, and not worry about when he leaves?"

"Sure. You could apply it to that."

"Huh." She scratched her chin. "I don't know if that'll work."

Aunt Debby laughed and patted her leg. "Go clean up Moondance. You don't have much time."

"Okay." Emily turned Moondance back toward the barn as she thought about what Aunt Debby had said, trying to decide whether she could really accept being around Sapphire and not riding him.

She'd almost decided she could . . . but when she walked past his stall with Moondance's tack after putting Moondance away and he stuck his head out and whickered at her . . .

"Oh, Sapphire." She dropped the tack on a hay bale and ran over and hugged him. "How can I possibly not ride you?" She unhooked his stall door to slip inside and play with him and—

"Emily!"

She jumped a mile and leaped back from the door, whirling toward her aunt, who was standing at the end of the aisle. Aunt Debby was wearing a pair of black pants and black boots, and her hair was blown dry, hanging around her shoulders in a soft cut, instead of up in a ponytail. She actually looked pretty.

"I was just—"

Aunt Debby tapped her watch. "We have to leave in fifteen minutes, Emily. You don't have time to be dawdling. Get in the house and change. We can't be late for Pa's funeral."

Emily grabbed Moondance's tack off the hay bale. "I promise I won't make us late. I can change really quickly." She hurried past Aunt Debby, pausing when she neared her. "Um, thanks for the lesson. It was awesome."

Aunt Debby smiled, even though there was a sadness in her eyes. "You're welcome. We'll do another one tomorrow. Now, go change."

"Right." Her heart racing at the thought of another jumping lesson tomorrow, Emily tossed Moondance's saddle and bridle in the tack room and sprinted down the aisle toward the house, determined not to upset Aunt Debby by making them late.

Emily took the fastest shower in history, and her hair was still dripping as she yanked on her skirt and blouse, the only nice clothes she'd brought with her. Her feet still bare, she ran in the bathroom and started blowing dry her hair, watching the time as she went. With three minutes to go, she shut off the hair dryer and bolted into the hall to head to her room. Only tights and shoes and then she'd be ready to go. As she rounded the corner, she saw her two little cousins sprint into her room, slamming the door shut behind them as they squealed.

What was up with that? Emily ran down the hall and shoved open her door to find them hanging out her window, shouting encouragement at someone. "What's going on?"

Caitlyn glanced back at Emily, her hair pulled back in two French braids with red bows on the ends of them. She was wearing a navy dress with cowboy boots. "Sapphire's out again."

"*What*?" Emily ran to the window in time to see Sapphire sprint down the driveway toward the road, his iron-shod feet crunching on the gravel. "Oh, *no*. He's going to get hit by a car!"

Uncle Rick shouted something, and she saw him jump into his truck in his tie and blue jeans and peel down the road after Sapphire while Aunt Debby ran into the barn yelling, "Alison, saddle my horse!"

"This is awesome," Kyle said as he leaned out the window. "We're going to be late for the funeral. Mom's going to be so mad!"

Emily looked at her watch and held her breath. Two minutes until they were supposed to leave.

Caitlyn frowned at Emily. "Mom said you were the last one in his stall. You didn't lock the stall door, did you?"

"Me? Of course I did." She hesitated with sudden dread. Had she locked it? She didn't remember. Aunt Debby had showed up and she'd left. Oh, *no*. Had she really let him out? Emily grabbed her tights and yanked them over her feet, her heart racing. "I'll go help them—"

"Your dad can ride?" Caitlyn sounded shocked.

"Of course he can't." Emily glanced out the window to see what Caitlyn was talking about, then her jaw dropped open as her dad went charging out of the barn at a dead gallop on a huge dark bay horse. He was perfectly balanced, his hands soft, his body smooth and motionless as he moved easily with the horse. Holy cow! She'd had no idea her dad could ride. Why hadn't he ever told her?

"He's good," Kyle said as her dad's horse galloped down the driveway, Aunt Debby following close behind him on another horse, yelling something at Emily's dad. She was still wearing her dress-up clothes, and her perfectly blown dry hair was flying behind her as they rode hard after Sapphire. Aunt Debby's body was rigid with fury, and Emily shrank back behind the drapes, wanting to crawl under her bed and never come out. What had she done?

Caitlyn and Kyle leaned farther out, trying to watch the action until all the horses disappeared from sight, then they both turned around to look at Emily. Kyle was grinning. "You're so busted."

Caitlyn's eyes were wide. "What if we miss the funeral?"

"Or what if Sapphire gets hurt or lost and Mom can't sell him?" Kyle added, a mischievous grin in his eyes. "We'll lose the farm, and it'll be all your fault."

Emily's stomach churned, and she grabbed her paddock boots and yanked them over her tights. "I'm going to help them. I'll ride Moondance and help get Sapphire. He'll come to me. I know he will."

Caitlyn's brown eyes became even larger. "Do you have permission to ride on your own yet?"

Emily hesitated. "Not specifically, no. Do I need it?"

"Oh, if you don't have permission, you'll be in soooo much trouble if you grab a horse and ride after them." Caitlyn gave a firm nod. "My mom never messes around when it comes to the horses. She'll ground you."

Emily frowned. "Ground me?"

"No riding. She did that to Alison just last month. No riding for three weeks."

"Oh." *Oh.* Emily hated the thought of not being allowed to ride at all. No chance of riding Sapphire?

Kyle grinned. "You should do it. You're already in trouble anyway, right? What's more trouble?"

Emily hesitated, her stomach lurching. Should she

help? Or hide? She thought of Sapphire racing toward the street and knew she had no choice. "I'm going!"

Kyle gave her a thumbs-up. "Cool."

Caitlyn shook her head. "Oh . . . you're going to be soooo sorry. Mom's not going to want you to stay here forever anymore."

"We aren't staying forever, anyway." Still in her skirt and tights, with her paddock boots untied, Emily raced out of the room and down the stairs, aware of Caitlyn and Kyle on her heels, jabbering loudly about how much trouble she was in and whether Aunt Debby would cry if they missed Grandpa's funeral.

Emily sprinted into the barn and bolted straight for the tack room, where she grabbed Moondance's tack, sweat dripping down her back underneath her nice white blouse. She jogged down the aisle, lugging the tack with her until she made it to Moondance's stall, with Caitlyn and Kyle still following her.

"So, I bet that Mom sends Emily home tonight," Kyle said to Caitlyn.

"Tonight? I bet she just grounds her. Makes her do chores for a month," Caitlyn says. "But she definitely won't let her near the horses. Letting Sapphire out *and* breaking the rules by taking a horse without permission . . . soooo much trouble."

Emily glared at them as she opened Moondance's door. "Will you guys please stop talking!"

"It's so much more fun to have you in trouble than me," Kyle said. "I'll be sad when she sends you home."

"No, I'm the one who will be sad," Caitlyn announced. "We never got a chance to play in my fort in the hay barn."

Emily felt sick as she threw the saddle over Moondance's back. She hated being in trouble. *Hated it*. But what else was she supposed to do? Let Sapphire get hit by a car?

"Oh!" Caitlyn jerked her head around and stared down the aisle. "I think they're back."

Emily paused and stuck her head out the door, and heard the easy thud of hoofbeats outside the barn. Not galloping. Walking. Then her dad's voice echoed through the barn. "He must have been tired from running around yesterday."

They'd caught Sapphire already? For a moment, Emily sagged with relief that he'd been brought back so quickly, and it didn't sound like he was hurt.

"It was really helpful having both of us to corner him," Aunt Debby said. "I'm impressed you can still ride. I thought I was going to have to ground you when I saw you get on that horse and tear out of here without my permission."

Her dad snorted. "I can still ride just fine."

"Barely. I was sure I'd be picking you up off the ground at any second. . . . Shoot! Look at the time!" Aunt Debby groaned. "I can't believe we're going to be late to Pa's funeral. He'd never forgive us."

"We're not going to be late," her dad said firmly. "We'll just hurry."

"They're coming!" Caitlyn shrieked. "You have to get the tack back before they realize you were going to steal Moondance!" Caitlyn grabbed the bridle, her cheeks flushing with excitement. "We have to beat her back to the tack room."

"Cool! A race!" Kyle jumped back as Emily threw herself out of the door and shoved it shut, making sure to bolt it carefully. Then she took off down the aisle after Caitlyn, who was waving furiously at her to hurry.

The *thunk* of horse hooves grew closer as they raced back to the tack room. Emily skidded around the corner, tripped on the door threshold, and crashed face-first into the saddle horse in the middle of the room.

Pain shot through her forehead, and she staggered to her feet as Kyle burst into laughter, holding his sides.

"Are you okay?" Caitlyn asked as she jumped up, trying to reach the bridle hook.

"Yeah, sort of." Blinking against the pain in her head, Emily grabbed the bridle from Caitlyn and threw it on the hook, then hoisted the saddle back onto its rack with a grunt.

Footsteps sounded outside the tack room, and she whirled to face the door as Aunt Debby stuck her head in. She was holding on to Sapphire, his ribs heaving and sweat drenching his neck and chest. His ears flicked forward when Emily saw him, but she didn't dare wave at him.

Her aunt's brow was furrowed, and her lips were in a tight line. Her perfect hairdo was now a mess, and she had horse slobber on her nice black pants. "Emily," she snapped. "Go outside and grab my horse from your dad. I want him cooled off and in his stall in less than three minutes." She shot a look at Emily's feet. "And you're not wearing paddock boots to the funeral. Go change. Kyle, go help Alison load up Max, and Caitlyn, go sit in the truck so you don't get any dirtier than you already are."

"I'm on it." Emily wiped her sweaty palms on her hands and sprinted past Aunt Debby, patting Sapphire's bum as she ran past, not wanting to be there when Kyle stopped laughing and explained to Aunt Debby what was so funny.

She was in so much trouble; she could tell. How could she have messed up so badly? Aunt Debby would never forgive her.

Ever.

*T*he silence was so unbearable, Emily felt like it
was crushing her. She and her dad were following
Uncle Rick's Suburban as he whizzed down the road,
the trailer containing Max clattering a little wildly. "I
said I was sorry," she said again.

Her dad sighed. "Em, I know you didn't mean to
let Sapphire out, but it's very upsetting to all of us to be
late to Pa's funeral."

She bit her lower lip against the tears stinging her
eyes. Her dad never got mad at her about anything.
They were on the same team, and he never got rattled.
But he was gripping the steering wheel so tightly that his
knuckles were white and his jaw was clenched. "They'll

wait for you, though. Won't they?" Emily asked.

"Probably." He said nothing else. Gave her no reassurances.

She wasn't used to the silent treatment from her dad, and she shifted in her seat. "Maybe I should just stay in the car. Since everyone's so mad at me."

Her dad shot her a look. "Emily, no one's mad at you. These things happen. We all know that."

"Everyone seems mad at me. Aunt Debby yelled at me three times, and even Uncle Rick snapped at me. And they made us take separate cars. We could have all fit in their Suburban."

"It's stressful. We're all upset already at the fact Pa died, and this adds to it. And it's good to give them a little space. It's a difficult time." He patted her knee and gave her a grim smile. "But I *will* be upset with you if you don't come to the funeral. He was your grandfather, and you need to be there."

Emily turned her head to stare out the window, watching the lush green pastures whiz by, wishing she was riding Sapphire through them instead of heading off to a funeral for a grandpa she'd never met, with the entire family hating her. "Can we at least sit by ourselves when we get there?"

"No. We'll sit with the family. It'll be fine."

Emily pressed her lips together; she knew it wouldn't be.

By the time they got to the reception after the funeral, Emily was so drained, she thought she'd never survive three hours of socializing.

The funeral had been just as awful as she thought it would be. Aunt Debby wouldn't even look at her, Kyle kept whispering that she was going to be sent back to New Jersey, and Emily felt really uncomfortable being around all these people who knew her grandfather while she didn't.

People kept standing up to tell stories about him, and everyone would laugh and cry at the memories, and she felt really out of place. She actually wanted to laugh a couple times, and even got sad because he sounded like he'd been a nice guy and she wished she'd known him, too . . . but then felt like a fraud since she hadn't even met him. She had no idea how she was supposed to act. And when she leaned over to ask her dad . . . she realized he was crying.

Her dad! Crying! Emily had almost started crying herself at the sight of the tears going down his cheeks. She'd never seen her dad cry. *Ever*. It scared her and made her feel even more awkward. Even when he put his arm around her shoulders and hugged her, she still felt weird. Like she didn't even know him anymore.

Emily sighed and leaned against a tree at the reception, watching all the people talk and laugh. There were tons of people there, which was actually nice. She was glad Grandpa had lots of friends. And his horse, Max, had even been invited, as Grandpa's best friend.

Emily glanced over at the old gray horse shoving his nose into the punch bowl as a bunch of kids shrieked with laughter. Aunt Debby and Uncle Rick had brought him to the reception and let him wander around the backyard, but Emily was too upset to truly appreciate how cool it was.

She watched Max move over and start munching the watermelon right off the platter, ignoring all the hugs everyone was giving him. One woman had even made him a new sheet that said MAX on it.

Emily took another bite of the cold cheese pizza she'd been nibbling on. The music was loud and upbeat (Caitlyn had identified it as country music), and everyone seemed determined to have a fun time in honor of how Grandpa would have wanted it. Aunt Debby and her dad still hadn't looked at her once. Her dad was too busy greeting all these people who used to be his friends, and Aunt Debby was sitting in the corner with a group of women who were giving her hugs.

It didn't help that Alison was hanging out in the shade with her friends, and even though Emily had walked by six times, Alison had never invited Emily to join them. Caitlyn and Kyle had gone off with their friends, leaving Emily alone with the tree.

Granted, it was a very cool pine tree that was about ten miles high, and she could smell the sap as she leaned against it, but still. She felt completely alone and out of place and desperately wanted to leave. She'd tried to apologize to Aunt Debby twice, and each time Aunt Debby had shaken her head and said they'd talk later.

Emily took a deep breath, wondering whether she should try again. She couldn't stand the thought of anyone being mad at her. Then she saw her dad walking toward her, and she could have almost cried with relief. "Dad!"

He threw his arm around her shoulders and hugged her against his side. "You doing all right, kiddo? I know this has been a long day."

"Yeah." Emily snuggled against him. "I'm sorry about Sapphire."

Her dad squeezed her shoulder. "It's okay, hon. They delayed the funeral for us, and it was a wonderful service. No harm done."

She looked at him. "Do you think Aunt Debby will forgive me? She wouldn't let me apologize."

He smiled. "It'll all be fine. She's emotional today, so just let her be for now, okay?"

"You're sure?"

"I'm sure," her dad said firmly, then they both looked up as someone yelled his name. It was a tall, blond man with a lined face and sunburned features. "Jack!" A huge smile split her dad's face. "You look good for an old guy!" He glanced back at Emily. "Do you mind if I run? He and I used to be great friends."

She shrugged and tried not to look miserable. She'd done enough to ruin the funeral, already, and she wasn't going to complain. "No, that's fine."

Her dad gave her a sympathetic look. "Uncle Rick's leaving now to deal with an emergency. He's taking my car back to the farm to get his truck and dropping off Caitlyn and Kyle. You want him to take you back, too?"

Emily perked up, her heart jumping with relief. "Would that be okay?"

"Of course." He hugged Emily and ruffled her hair. "Thanks for coming, Em. I was proud to have you here with me."

She buried her face in his jacket as she hugged him back. "It wasn't so bad."

"Okay, then." Her dad kissed the top of her head

and gave her a gentle shove toward the door. "Go catch Uncle Rick before he leaves. I'll be home later."

"Okay!" Emily didn't waste time sprinting for the door, so no one could see her relief at the thought of escaping.

The ride back to the farm had been completely uncomfortable. Uncle Rick, Caitlyn, and Kyle had talked about Grandpa the entire time. Caitlyn had even cried and so had Uncle Rick. Emily had felt like a complete intruder and had been desperate to get out of the truck when they arrived at the farm. She'd run inside to change into her jeans and paddock boots and felt better almost right away just being in her real clothes.

Emily jogged down the stairs, then stopped on the bottom step when she heard Kyle and Caitlyn talking about Grandpa in the other room, *Saddle Club* blaring on the TV in the background.

"Emily? Is that you? Come watch *Saddle Club*," Caitlyn called out.

Emily tensed at the thought of going in there and listening to more stories that she couldn't share, stories that made her feel like an outsider. She hadn't belonged all day, and she needed to see Sapphire. To go to the one place where she could be herself and it would be okay. "I'm going to the barn."

"Oh, cool." Caitlyn popped her head out of the door. "We'll come out as soon as *Saddle Club*'s over. About five minutes. Then we can hang out all afternoon. I can show you this tree house that Grandpa made for us, okay?"

"Um, yeah." Emily didn't especially want to hang out with her cousins, reliving memories of the grandfather she didn't know, and who she'd never know now. She needed private time with Sapphire, time to find her space. The minute she got out there to see him, Caitlyn and Kyle would be there, too. In her space.

Emily thought of Sapphire's shiny coat and his dark brown eyes and knew she couldn't share him. Not right now. Just for a short while, she needed him.

Her gaze flicked to the living room. There was only one way she could get Sapphire to herself for a little bit. Did she dare? Aunt Debby would be furious . . . but if she went quickly, she could make it back before they even returned from the funeral.

Her dad would understand. He always told her to follow her heart, and her heart knew what she needed right now.

She needed Sapphire.

*E*mily whirled on the stairs and vaulted back up the steps to her bedroom. She grabbed her riding helmet off the nightstand and sprinted down the stairs two at a time, moving too fast for Caitlyn or Kyle to intercept her. She grabbed an apple out of the kitchen, then leaped off the back porch as the screen door slammed behind her. She sprinted into the barn, and ran all the way to the tack room.

Gasping for air, she grabbed Sapphire's tack, jogged down the aisle to his stall, then propped it against the wall. Her hands were shaking with excitement as she yanked his door open.

She sighed with delight the moment she saw his

beautiful black face turned toward her and felt all her loneliness fade away. His neck was glossy and shining, curved with muscle, and the three white shavings stood out in his lustrous black tail. "Sapphire," she breathed, in awe over his beauty once again.

He whickered, then immediately walked over to her and pressed his warm nose into her hand. She grinned and opened her palm so he could eat the apple. As he munched, she laid her cheek on his head between his eyes, closing her eyes at his soft hair on her face. "You're the best."

Sapphire gave her a hard nudge and sent her flying so she landed on her butt. She peered up at him, then laughed when he shook his head and began nuzzling her hair, as if searching for treats she might have hidden behind her ear. "Okay, let's go. We have to hurry. We don't have long until everyone gets back."

She kissed his nose, then hopped up. She ran a quick brush over him, picked out his feet, then threw the saddle on his back. As soon as she started to do up his girth, he took a few steps, and she remembered what Aunt Debby has said about hooking him up to the cross ties. "Shoot. You're supposed to be learning to be good."

He swung his head around to look at her, his big

brown eyes regarding her as if begging her not to tie him up.

She sighed and patted his nose. "Okay, but swear you won't tell, okay?"

He bobbed his head as if in agreement, then started munching on his hay while she finished tightening the girth. Then she took hold of the bridle, and he stood patiently while she slipped it on, unlike Moondance.

She grabbed her helmet, put on her leather riding gloves, then peered out the door, her heart pounding with excitement and nervousness.

No one was around. Everyone from the barn was still at the reception.

As she led him out the door of the stall, the *plop* of his iron-shod feet on the cement sounded loudly. Emily winced with each step, glancing nervously around to see if anyone had come running.

But no one appeared as they reached the door to the outside. She led Sapphire up to the ring, gathered the reins, then climbed on the middle fence rail so she could reach the stirrup.

She paused with her toe in the stirrup. Was she really going to do this? She'd never blatantly broken a rule before.

Sapphire swung his head around to look at her, his white blaze bright in the afternoon sunshine. Then he stomped his foot impatiently.

"Okay, I'm coming." She took a deep breath then swung her other leg over his back.

She grinned as she settled into the saddle, feeling his massive body underneath her. He was all muscle and strength and beauty.

And for this moment, he was hers.

10

The moment they were out of sight of the house, Emily nudged Sapphire into a trot. He obliged immediately, sliding into the smoothest trot she'd ever experienced. He moved like silk, his gait effortless and powerful.

She sighed with delight as she sank deeper into the saddle, feeling each step he took, listening to the sounds of his hooves as they thudded softly into the grass. His muscles rippled under his coat, and sun reflected off him, making him glisten. The sun beat down on her arms, and she could practically smell it heating up the earth, filling her with light.

A bird flew in front of Sapphire, and he jerked his

head up in surprise, jarring her. But she patted his neck, and he settled right down, giving her time to look around at the woods and fields surrounding them as far as she could see.

Surrounded only by nature and the smell of wetness and spring, no one could tell either of them what to do.

She lifted her arms toward the sky and raised her face to the warm sun. "I'm free!" she shouted to the world. "Free!"

Sapphire broke into a canter, and she let him, basking in the feel of his body coiling beneath her. He was solid power, unlike Rhapsody, who was more like refined elegance and grace. Sapphire was—

He squealed suddenly and bolted.

Emily yelped and grabbed for his mane as she almost fell off, barely managing to right herself as he galloped across the fields. His head was extended, his ears back against the wind, his feet pounding on the dirt.

Emily caught her balance, then moved into a half-seat and stretched out low across his neck, the wind whipping her face and nearly taking her breath away. Exhilaration rushed through her and she started laughing, overwhelmed by the sheer power and freedom of the experience. This was her moment. Pure joy.

Sapphire stretched even farther as he increased his

speed, and she clung to him, not even trying to control him or slow him down. Just letting him take her for the most amazing ride of her life. Running from what they'd left behind, running toward whatever surprises awaited them. No plans, no rules, no feeling bad. Just completely in the moment.

"Woo-hoo!" She let her cry disappear into the wind, absorbed by nature and the fresh air filling her lungs with freedom and energy.

They ran, nothing in the world but the two of them and the wind, the thud of Sapphire's hooves on the damp earth, the sound of his breathing as he raced the wind.

Finally, Sapphire began to slow to a less frenzied gallop, and she sank back into the saddle, breathing almost as hard as he was. She leaned forward and draped herself across his neck, wrapping her arms around his muscled neck as far as she could reach, pressing her face against his sweaty coat, bouncing with each stride. "Thank you for letting me come along. Now I know why you escape so much. It's brilliant out here." She nuzzled his mane. "Don't tell Aunt Debby, but I love you."

He snorted and shied sideways, and she grinned, knowing that they would forever have the bond of this ride, of sharing the flight from reality to a world where they weren't bound by anyone or anything. "I can't imagine how I'll ever go back to dressage after this," she told him. "This is what riding is all about."

She realized they were heading toward some woods, so she sat back in the saddle a bit and took up a firmer hold on the reins. She didn't want him to gallop into the woods and run into a tree, but she also wasn't ready to turn around yet.

She had a feeling she'd never be ready to go back.

He slowed to an easy canter, and she sighed with delight as she settled into the saddle. He was so comfortable, his gait so smooth that her upper body barely moved with his rhythm.

She noticed a small stream in front of them, and started to slow Sapphire to a trot so they could cross it without falling on the rocks. But Sapphire grabbed the bit from her and increased his speed as his ears pricked forward, toward the stream.

"Easy, boy," she crooned. "Whoa, whoa, whoa," she softly chanted to him as she tugged the reins, trying to coax him into slowing down. He didn't, and at the last second, she realized he was going to jump the stream.

Excitement shot through her, and she gave him his head, rising into her half-seat as his feet took off.

"Ack!" He exploded into the air, and she got left

behind, totally not prepared for the powerful lurch of his body as he leaped forward. She lost her grip on the reins, and her feet flew out of the stirrups. Then he landed with a thump that jarred her forward onto his neck. She grabbed for his mane as she started to slide down his neck toward the ground, her heart racing as Sapphire increased his speed.

Then he dropped his head and did a little buck, and she catapulted off him onto the ground. She threw up her arms to brace herself and crashed hard. Pain shot up her ankle and shattered through her body.

She groaned as she rolled to a stop, unable to move through the pain. The thud of Sapphire's hooves faded and her heart dropped as she opened her eyes and looked around.

He was gone.

11

*P*anic shot through her and she rolled to her stomach, yelping as fresh pain exploded in her ankle. "Sapphire!"

Nothing but the rustle of leaves and the trickle of water.

"Sapphire!" She grabbed a small tree and pulled herself to her feet, standing on one foot as she scanned the woods for a black horse. "Sapphire!"

No response. He was gone, just as he'd taken off those other times.

Tears filled her eyes. "Sapphire," she begged. "Please come back."

A squirrel ran partway down a tree trunk, chattering

at her while his little tail twitched, as if he were laughing.

"Go away," she muttered, clenching her teeth against the pain as she hopped toward the stream and back the way they'd come.

She didn't want to go home without him, but she didn't know what else to do. Maybe she'd find him on the way.

She made it to the edge of the water, then frowned at the smooth rocks under the surface. No way could she hop across those. She touched the toe of her injured foot to the ground, then winced and yanked it back.

She looked around and saw a large stick nearby. She crawled over to it, then used it to leverage herself to her feet again. Using the stick for balance and support, she hopped back over to the stream and wedged the stick down between the rocks.

She leaned on it carefully, testing it. When it didn't slip, she put all her weight on it and then hopped into the water, landing on a round rock just beneath the surface. The cold seeped in through her boots, her muscles tightened to keep her balance, and she hopped again. And again.

Then she moved the stick forward a few feet, wedged it tightly between two rocks, and hopped again. The stick slipped and flew out of her hand, and she screeched as she fell into the cold water, her ankle screaming with pain as she smacked it against a rock.

Water streaming down her face, she managed to haul herself back up to her knees and crawl out of the stream, the rocks digging into her knees and hands.

She pulled herself up the bank, unable to keep the tears from creeping out of her eyes, and flopped down on her belly on the grass, her body shaking with exhaustion and pain.

A minute of rest. That was all she needed.

Just a minute and then she'd keep going.

By six o'clock that evening, the farm was in chaos.

Caitlyn and Kyle reported Emily had gone missing when the adults arrived home, and Emily's dad had been the one to realize that Sapphire was also gone. Aunt Debby had been furious and worried that Emily was going to be in trouble riding Sapphire out in the woods.

Emily's dad had spent the next hour trying to calm his sister down, taking responsibility for allowing Emily to do whatever she wanted, and reassuring her that Emily was a great rider, even if she wasn't experienced at jumping. But after four hours had passed with no sign of either of them, even he had started to get worried.

By six fifteen, they'd assembled on horses in the driveway with walkie-talkies, since cell phones didn't work that far out from town. Emily's dad, Alison, Aunt Debby, and even Uncle Rick, who had canceled his last appointments for the day, all mounted. A girl from the barn named Meredith joined them.

Aunt Debby gave instructions. "Meredith and Alison, you two stay together and once it starts to get dark, you both head home. I want your horses in their stalls before dark, okay?"

The girls nodded, and Aunt Debby turned to the adults. "The rest of us will split up." She created search parameters for everyone.

Aunt Debby patted Emily's dad's arm as she swung her mount past him. "We'll find her." Then she whirled her horse and bolted up the path toward the extensive lands behind the barn. Emily's dad nudged his horse into action and tore after her, his throat dry.

Emily groaned and rolled onto her back in the field, too tired to crawl any farther, and she'd lost track of which way was home. When Sapphire had bolted, she'd stopped paying attention and just enjoyed the ride.

Not her smartest move.

All she was hoping for at this point was a road, so she

could flag down a car, but there weren't even any roads. The vast expanse of fields that yesterday had seemed so beautiful just seemed huge and scary now. And lonely.

She pressed her hands to her face against the swell of tears. She was wet and cold, and in so much pain she'd taken off her sweatshirt and tied it around her ankle to try to immobilize it and cushion it from getting knocked.

It had helped a little bit but not enough.

She stared up at the sky, realizing the sun was beginning to set, and she shuddered. Alone out here in the *dark*? She moaned and rolled back to her knees and started to crawl again, then heard a faint noise. Had that been someone yelling her name? She jumped up, careful to not put any weight on her injured foot, her heart pounding with hope.

She held her breath and listened intently.

Silence.

Her throat tightened, and she was just about to give up when she heard it again. It was *definitely* someone yelling her name. "I'm here!" she shouted. "I'm right here!" She waved her arms, not knowing what direction to face. "I'm here! Help!"

She kept turning around as someone yelled her name again, and then she saw it. A silhouetted figure on a horse at the other end of the field. "Right here!" It was too far away to tell who it was, and she didn't even care if it was Aunt Debby. "Here!" Waving her arms, she hopped toward the horse, then stopped when the horse spun in her direction and started galloping toward her.

Relief made tears well in her eyes, and her legs gave out. She plunked down on her butt, unable to stop crying as Uncle Rick reined in beside her and vaulted off his horse, a liver chestnut she recognized from the farm as Mystic, a full sister to Moondance. "Emily! Are you all right?"

She tried to answer, but she was crying too hard, so she just nodded and pointed to her ankle. Uncle Rick ignored the ankle and swept her up in a giant hug, and she hugged him back as tightly as she could. After a minute, he pulled back slightly so he could look at her face. "You're okay?"

"I hurt my ankle."

"Other than that?"

"I'm wet."

He grinned and sat her back on the grass. "Well, I think we can probably take care of both of those problems." He paused to pull a walkie-talkie off his belt and reported in that he'd found her and she was fine.

Her dad was so panicked that he made her talk into

the walkie-talkie before he'd believe Uncle Rick, and Emily felt guilty, realizing how much she'd upset him. "I'm sorry, Dad. I didn't mean to scare you."

"No, hon, I'm just glad you're safe." His voice was trembling, and Emily felt awful.

"I miss you, Dad."

"Oh, hon, I miss you, too. You're really okay?"

"I'm really okay."

"Thank God." There was a scuffling noise, then her dad said, "Aunt Debby wants to talk to you."

"No, wait—"

"Is Sapphire okay?"

Emily felt her cheeks turn red, and she stared at the ground. "I fell off," she mumbled. "He ran away."

"What?" Aunt Debby's voice crackled over the walkie-talkie. "I can't hear you."

Uncle Rick put his hand on Emily's head and gently patted it as he took the walkie-talkie from her hand. "Sapphire took off," he told his wife. "You and Scott should keep looking for him. I'll take care of Emily."

He signed off after agreeing to keep in touch and then unwrapped the sweatshirt from Emily's ankle, his touch so gentle it barely hurt.

"I'm in trouble, aren't I?"

He glanced at her, his face kind. "Aunt Debby just

worries about your safety. That's all. She knows what can happen around horses."

"It was a onetime thing. It's not like I fall off all the time—"

Uncle Rick raised his brows. "Let's concentrate on your ankle first, okay? We'll talk about the rest when everyone's back at the farm."

"Can't we stay out here all night?" Now that Uncle Rick was with her, it seemed like a better place to be than back at the house getting in trouble.

Uncle Rick laughed. "It won't be that bad, I promise."

"I'll be grounded, though." Her eyes started to fill up again at the thought.

"Very possible," he agreed, then he set his fingers on her ankle and began to probe.

For the next five minutes, she forgot about everything except how much her ankle hurt.

Ten minutes later, Rick sat back on his heels after rewrapping her ankle with white tape he'd brought along in his emergency medical kit. "I'd have to take X-rays, but I think it's just sprained."

"Just? It kills."

He nodded. "Sprains can hurt more than broken ankles." He stood up. "Let's get you home."

Emily couldn't go yet. She had to ask. "Are you still mad about Sapphire escaping before the funeral?" She swallowed. "I'm really sorry."

Uncle Rick ruffled her hair. "Oh, Emily, no one's mad at you for that. It happens. The timing was bad, so maybe we got more upset than we would have otherwise." He squatted in front of her and put his hands on her shoulders. "Look at me."

She dragged her gaze off the ground and focused on his face.

He smiled. "I promise you, no one's mad about Sapphire escaping. It happens, especially with him. Okay?"

She felt her shoulders sag, and her belly began to uncurl. "Okay."

"Good." He bent to sweep her up in his arms. "Come on. You can ride with me, and we'll get you home, where I can do a better job on that ankle."

She stifled a squawk of pain as he helped her slide into the saddle, then swung up behind her, the two of them barely fitting in the saddle. He wrapped one arm around her to steady her, then eased Mystic into a gentle canter, heading in the complete opposite direction she'd been going in, and she realized she'd been heading away from the farm instead of toward it. She shuddered at the thought of what would have happened if Uncle Rick hadn't found her—

"Rick!" Aunt Debby's voice crackled through the walkie-talkie. "We've got an emergency! Horse down! We're about a mile west, by the old sawmill. Get over here now!"

Emily tensed as she jerked upright. "Horse down? Sapphire's hurt?" Oh, no! What had she done?

"I'm on my way." Uncle Rick whirled Mystic around and urged her into a gallop, his arm tight around Emily to keep her from falling off as Mystic bounded across the uneven ground.

Emily clutched tight to him, feeling sick at the thought of Sapphire down. Hurt.

Because of her.

Then they got to the top of a hill, she saw Aunt Debby and her dad, and she realized she'd been totally wrong.

*I*t wasn't Sapphire who was hurt, she realized with a
sob of relief.

Sapphire was standing over a dark bay horse that
was on his belly. The injured horse had his front legs
out in front as he tried to pull himself to his feet. He
had a big blaze down the front of his face and two white
rear socks.

Aunt Debby was holding the injured horse's halter,
and her dad was shoving at his butt, both of them trying to help the horse stand.

Mystic thundered down the hill just as the horse
managed to stagger to his feet, rocking dangerously
back and forth once he made it.

Aunt Debby shouted, and Emily's dad brought his horse, which she realized was Moondance, around to the side, using her as a brace to hold up the other horse. Moondance planted her feet and leaned into the injured horse, clearly accustomed to being used to do exactly that.

"What's wrong?" Mystic skidded to a stop and Uncle Rick vaulted to the ground, yanking his medical kit out of his saddlebag.

"Bad leg. Deep wound on his side—" Aunt Debby stopped talking suddenly and looked at Emily. "Go back to the top of the hill and wait for us. I don't want you to see this."

But Emily didn't move. She was too shocked by the sight of the injured horse. He was so thin she could see all his bones, and his head hung low with exhaustion. She slid off Mystic and hobbled to the injured animal, hugging his face to her belly and patting him.

He let out a huge sigh that made him shudder, then pressed his head into her. Sapphire lowered his head, and she kissed his nose, so relieved to see him.

Emily wrapped her arms around both the injured horse and Sapphire and looked at the adults, who were ignoring her again, clustered around the injured horse's back left side, all of them looking really, really serious. "Is he okay?"

Emily's dad finally looked at her, and his face was grim. "He's hurt badly, Em, and no one took care of him."

"Well, why not? Who was supposed to take care of him?"

Aunt Debby turned her head and gave Emily a thoughtful look. "Now that is a very good question." Her eyes narrowed. "I intend to find that out."

Emily's dad glanced at Aunt Debby. "I'll head back to the barn and pick up the trailer. He'll never make it back there on his own."

Aunt Debby nodded as Uncle Rick bent over, inspecting the wound. "Hurry."

Emily's dad gestured at Emily. "Ride Mystic. I'll take Sapphire."

"Sapphire? But—" Emily paused as her dad gave her a leg up onto Mystic, then she watched her dad swing onto Sapphire's back and grab the tattered reins to turn him back into the woods. The stirrup banged against her ankle and she flinched, so she quickly flipped the stirrups over Mystic's withers, crossing them so they'd stay out of the way while she rode. There was no way she'd be able to ride with her feet in the stirrups. That kind of pressure on her ankle would be unbearable.

Her dad frowned. "You okay to ride?"

"I don't want her seeing this," Aunt Debby repeated. "Take her with you."

Emily instinctively glanced over her shoulder at the injured horse, whose head was hanging so low his chin was almost on the ground. He was holding his right back leg completely off the ground, and his front feet were splayed for balance. He looked like he was going to topple over right there.

"Come on," her dad said, gently turning Mystic's head so she followed him. "We need to get a van for him."

Emily felt her heart tighten for the horse as she let her dad lead her back up the hill she and Uncle Rick had just ridden down. "He doesn't look very good."

Her dad looked back at her. "No, he doesn't. Are you sure you're okay to ride?"

"Yeah." Emily finally tore her gaze off the horse and nudged Mystic into a canter beside Sapphire, too upset to be jealous that her dad got to ride him. She winced each time her ankle banged against Mystic's side, but refused to tell her dad to stop. Not with that horse looking so unhappy. "Aren't you supposed to tell me he's going to be fine?"

"I wish I could, sweets. I wish I could. But I don't think he is."

Emily had to fight back tears for most of the ride back to the house.

It was barely dawn the next morning when Emily sat on Moondance beside her dad, who was riding Spartacus, the huge dark bay horse he'd ridden yesterday when he'd chased after Sapphire.

Uncle Rick had put a walking cast on her ankle, which helped a lot. Her ankle was protected, and she could ride without unbearable pain, as long as she didn't use stirrups. Emily had thought you didn't cast for sprains, but apparently if they were bad enough, you did. She could put a little weight on her ankle, but she still limped and it throbbed whenever she stepped on it, but Uncle Rick had assured her it would heal up quickly.

Emily and her dad were at the spot where the injured horse had been found, and they were going to follow his tracks to find out where he came from. They'd decided to call the horse Trooper, because he'd somehow managed to drag himself along on three legs, like a super trooper.

Uncle Rick and Aunt Debby were staying at the barn, unable to leave him alone, and Alison was managing the barn for them.

Apparently, Emily's dad was the best tracker in the family—who knew? So he was in charge of finding where Trooper had come from, and he'd brought Emily with him.

Everyone seemed too freaked out about Trooper to remember that Emily had broken the rules yesterday when she'd stolen Sapphire, but she had no doubt that she'd be in trouble soon enough.

But she believed Uncle Rick that no one was mad about Sapphire escaping before the funeral, so she felt much better about that. It was one thing to get in trouble for knowingly breaking the rules, but it felt much worse to get in trouble for doing something she hadn't meant to do.

This morning she'd managed to slip unnoticed into Sapphire's stall while everyone was looking in on Trooper, who Aunt Debby still wouldn't let her see. Sapphire had been happy to see her, and she'd checked him carefully for injuries and had been horrified to see swelling around his left front ankle.

She'd told her dad, who had told her to wrap it for support, and leave it for when Uncle Rick had time to deal with him.

Her stomach hadn't stopped hurting since.

"There." Her dad pointed. "See the broken bushes?

He came through there."

Emily frowned and bent down to inspect the blackberry bush. Some of the branches were definitely broken. "How do you know that's not from Sapphire?"

"I'm guessing, because it wouldn't have made sense for Sapphire to be coming from that direction. Let's go."

Her dad leading the way, they slowly made their way through the woods and fields, following hoofprints, broken branches, and half-eaten vegetation.

The sun was high in the late morning when her dad reined in Spartacus. "There we go."

She followed his gaze and gasped as she saw what he was looking at. It was a huge stable, with lots of stalls that opened out into a tiny ring with broken fences, rusted cars, and a big pile of garbage. The horses were up to their ankles in mud, their coats caked, and all of them were so thin she could see their hip bones sticking out. The stench of manure and dirty stalls stung her nostrils. She covered her mouth with her hand. "Oh, *no*. Those poor horses! No wonder Trooper ran away!"

Her dad muttered a word she'd never heard him use before, then he clucked Spartacus into a gallop, riding straight for the barn.

Emily recovered herself and galloped after him.

* * *

"Hey! Who's in charge here?" Her dad slammed Spartacus to a stop just outside the front door to the falling-down barn, leaped off him, and charged inside.

Emily caught up and grabbed Spartacus's reins as he started to wander off. She could hear her dad shouting and doors slamming inside. Clenching the reins of both horses, she tugged them into a broken paddock, yanked off their tack and let them go, using the reins of one of the bridles to hold the gate shut, wincing at the rank odor drifting from inside the barn. There was a loud crash from inside, making Emily jump. "Dad? Everything okay?"

He shouted another word she'd never heard him use, and she sprinted for the barn, her heart racing in terror. "Dad!" She made it only three steps before she caught her cast and fell, pain screaming through her leg. Gritting her teeth against the throbbing in her ankle, she pulled herself to her feet and limped toward the barn as fast as she could. "Dad!"

13

When Emily got inside, her dad was yelling into a pay phone, sweat trickling down his forehead. "At least thirty horses! Call the cops, call 911 and get over here with the van and the trailer. We have to get them out!" He slammed down the phone and whirled toward Emily, his face red and the veins in his neck bulging. "Aunt Debby's on her way with the van. We're taking these horses out."

Her mouth dropped open. "We're stealing them?"

"Hey! What are you doing on my property?"

Emily spun around to see a tall, lanky man with long hair in a ratty ponytail slouch around the corner. He was wearing torn overalls and a cowboy hat and was sucking on a red Popsicle.

Her dad's eyes narrowed, and he seemed to swell to twice his regular size. "Is this your barn?" His voice was deep and rumbling with an intensity Emily had never heard him use. "Are these your horses?"

The man nodded. "What's it to you?"

Her dad shouted, and charged at the man.

"Dad!" Emily screamed as her dad tackled the man, shoving him through an open stall door that was flooded with gross, black water. The man went flying and landed with a huge *sploosh* as muddy water exploded up into the air and sloshed against the walls of the stall. Her dad slammed the door shut, shoved the bolt home, then grabbed a lead shank and tied it shut.

"Hey!" The man let out an outraged roar, and there was the sound of splashing as he fell, then he was at the stall door, his hands grabbing the bars. Black water was streaming down his face, and he looked like he had a chunk of manure wedged between the top of his ear and his head. "You can't lock me up!" He shook the door then slipped and went down with a yelp and another splash.

Emily couldn't help but stand and gawk as her dad double-checked his knot, then turned to face her, his mouth grim. "Okay, Em. Let's go round up these horses and start to bring them out front for Aunt Debby."

She stared at the stall as the man scrambled to his feet again and started shaking the door and shouting. "You're going to leave him there?"

Her dad glanced over his shoulder. "Yeah. Why? You think I should toss some manure in there with him?"

Emily giggled. "Probably." A horrible odor began to drift in her direction, and she pulled her shirt up over her nose. "Is that coming from the stall? What is it?"

"It's him. He stinks." Her dad grabbed a few lead shanks. "Grab whatever you can find. Halters, lead shanks. Anything. I'm going to start retrieving the horses. You find what you can and bring it to me." And then he took off at a run to the back of the barn.

Trying to ignore the owner still yelling at her dad, Emily hobbled over to a nearby trunk. She yanked it open, saw two little eyes staring at her, and screamed. She leaped back as a tiny little mouse skittered away, disappearing into a hole in the wall. She winced and bit her lip as she tried to catch her breath both from the scare and the throbbing in her ankle. "Dad?" Her voice was embarrassingly shaky. "Why don't I wait outside?"

"Here." Her dad was suddenly behind her. "Take this horse out front." He thrust a lead shank in her hand, grabbed three that were sitting in the trunk, and took off.

Emily stared at the horse he'd handed her, her heart tightening when she realized she could see all his ribs through his ragged brown-and-white coat. He looked like a white horse that someone had throw brown paint on, or she suspected that's what he'd look like once he got a bath. "Oh, *sweetie*." She hugged him, then gently tugged the lead shank, leading him slowly across the barn floor, trying not to step in the piles of manure and mud.

The horse lifted his head to look at the shouting owner as they passed him. The man grabbed the bars and yelled at the horse. The horse suddenly pinned his ears and charged at the door, jerking the lead shank out of Emily's hands. The horse bared his huge teeth, and the man screamed and leaped back from the door as the horse slammed his teeth down, grazing the tips of his fingers. "He bit me!"

"You deserve it!" Emily grinned as she gathered up the lead shank. "Good boy. Just for that, you can have all the hay you want when we get you home." The horse faked for the door again, and the man jumped away, then he yelped, and there was a splash as he fell into the muddy water again.

Emily patted the horse's neck as she led him outside, clunking awkwardly along in her cast. "I think I'm going to name you Jaws because you're so brilliant with your teeth." They stepped out into the bright sun, and Jaws stopped, blinking against the bright light, as if he'd never been outside before. "Oh, you poor baby."

He dropped his head and pressed it against her hip, as if to hide from the bright sun, and she scratched behind his ears, wincing at the thick layer of dirt on his coat. It ground under her fingernails, gritty and hard. "I'm so giving you a bath when we get home—"

A siren wailed suddenly, and Jaws jerked his head up and began to dance. Emily tried to calm him as a police car whizzed down the driveway, bouncing over the ruts, the blue lights flashing and the siren wailing so loud she flinched. Right behind the police car was the Running Horse Ridge van.

The police car stopped, the van screeched to a halt, and Aunt Debby was out of the truck and sprinting toward Emily before the cops had even gotten their doors open. "Oh, Emily! This poor horse! Are there more?"

"Yeah, in back. My dad's—"

But Aunt Debby was already racing past her, and she let out a loud screech once she got into the barn.

And then she was shouting, and Emily could hear her slamming something against wood. Emily grinned at Jaws. "I think she found the owner."

The cops jumped out and hurried past her, shouting at Aunt Debby to calm down.

Uncle Rick came tearing up the driveway behind Aunt Debby, driving a pickup with a two-horse trailer. He jumped out and ran up to Emily. He barely nodded to her before he started running his hands over Jaws's legs and checking him out.

"His name's Jaws," she told him.

Uncle Rick muttered something under his breath then stood up. "I think he's good to go. Load him up."

"Load him up?" One of the cops came outside. "You can't just take him."

Uncle Rick set his hands on his hips and glowered, looking completely tough and intimidating. "Look at this horse. Look at him!"

The cop looked and he paled.

"Now tell me I can't take him," Uncle Rick growled. "I dare you."

"I gotta call my chief." The cop ran over to his car and dove into the front seat as another siren began to scream in the distance.

Emily grinned at Uncle Rick. "That was great."

He shot her a brief smile. "I get mad when people mess with horses. You know how to drop the ramp and load him up?"

"I do."

He nodded, glancing at the barn, where Aunt Debby's voice rang out as she shouted something at the police officer who was still in there. "If Jaws gives you any trouble, stop and wait for us. But if you can get him loaded, great."

"No problem—"

But Uncle Rick was already running into the barn.

Emily waved at the cop as she led Jaws by the cruiser. He glanced at her but didn't try to stop her. Who would, with the way Uncle Rick had glared at him?

Jaws stood patiently as she loosened the ramp and lowered it, but before she'd gotten him into the trailer, two more police cars showed up. The cops ran right past her into the barn, leaving the lights flashing. Jaws started to prance again, and she had to walk him in a circle to calm him before trying to load him.

By the time she finally got him loaded, her dad came out with two more horses, Aunt Debby behind him leading three more. All the horses were so skinny she could see their bones, and three of them had nasty-looking wounds on their backs. "Emily!" Aunt Debby said. "Drop the ramp on the big van. We're loading up these guys." There was a cop right behind her, and he was frowning.

"Debby, I don't like you taking these horses like this. The owner's throwing a fit."

Emily's dad and Aunt Debby both whirled around to glare at the cop. "For heaven's sake, Jesse," Aunt Debby snapped. "Write up the seizure form that the county's taking the horses due to neglect, write me down as guardian, and stop getting in my way."

"I'll pay any fees for paperwork," Emily's dad added. "Just get it done."

"Do it." Another cop showed up behind Jesse, and she had an air of authority. "The owner just tried to knock out an officer with a water bucket, so we're arresting him and taking his horses."

Aunt Debby flashed the cop a grin. "Thanks, Linda."

Linda shrugged. "I don't like people who mistreat animals, and I really don't like people who try to drown my officers in nasty water. I'll make sure you get temporary custody." She walked to the van, grabbed the ramp, and hauled it out. "And I'll help you take them away."

"Great." Aunt Debby handed a lead shank to Emily. "We're saving this horse until the end. She's too upset by all the noise. I need you to take her on a nice walk away from the noise and let her calm down. I'll call when we're ready. It'll be at least an hour, maybe more."

"Sure thing." Emily grabbed the lead shank and looked at the horse, gasping when she realized the horse was hugely pregnant, her sides so distended she looked like she'd swallowed two elephants and a hippo for lunch. She was a light brown, but the exact color was hard to tell because the mud was so thick on her coat. Her legs were coated with shiny, wet mud, as if she'd been standing in it up to her ankles, and her ribs were sticking out. Her head was up, the whites of her eyes showing, and her nostrils were flaring. "Oh, you poor thing."

Another van turned into the driveway, and Aunt Debby waved. "It's Judi and Mark. They're going to help us transport."

The mare snorted as the van approached, her eyes rolling back in her head. Emily quickly turned the horse's head to the right and led her away from the barn. The mare kept dancing, her breath coming short and fast as she staggered to keep her balance. "Okay, sweetie, you need to calm down." Emily patted her neck, wincing at how thin it was. "I'm sure you feel awful right now and everything, so I'm going to call you Precious, because that's what you are, even if your owner didn't treat you right."

Precious snorted and jerked her head as one of the horses clattered up the ramp into the van. Emily started to worry that the mare's skinny legs wouldn't survive if Precious kept jumping around, so she started to sing to her. Precious swung her head around to look at Emily, then her ribs expanded with a huge sigh and her head dropped down in total exhaustion.

"There you go," Emily sang, making up a soothing tune. "Now we'll find a place for you to rest while we're waiting, waiting, waiting." She almost laughed at how bad the song was, but Precious seemed to be listening, so she kept talking and singing as she led Precious away from the frenzy to a shady tree to await her turn.

Two and a half hours later, Emily helped her dad lift the ramp on the trailer, latching it shut behind Precious. Emily wiped the sweat off her brow as she looked around at the now-empty barn. All the horses except Precious were now at Running Horse Ridge, getting cleaned and fed and checked on by Uncle Rick and Aunt Debby. The cops were gone, the owner had been carted off to jail, and the humane society had come down to document the condition of all the animals. Judi and Mark, the neighbors who had brought their van to help transport the horses, had offered to foster some of the horses, but Uncle Rick and Aunt Debby had insisted on taking all of them until they could check them over.

Running Horse Ridge was packed now, and some of the healthier horses had been turned out in the back pastures to run so the injured ones could be put in stalls.

Only Precious was left. It was almost over.

Emily's dad walked around to the back of the trailer and checked the latches. "All set?"

"All set." Emily was so tired, and her clothes and cast were covered in dirt. She was worried that the plastic bag she'd wrapped around the cast wasn't doing enough to keep it from getting drenched with mud and manure and other stuff she didn't want in her bed.

"Let's go, then."

Emily limped over to the front of the truck and climbed into the cab. Her dad eased the truck into gear and slowly started the tires rolling, so as not to jar Precious. They'd had to shift the divider to the side so she'd fit in the trailer, and even then, it had been tight.

Emily let her head drop back against the seat and closed her eyes. "I'm so tired."

The truck rolled to a gentle stop at the end of the driveway. "How are you holding up?" her dad asked.

Emily opened her eyes. "I'm a little freaked out," she admitted. "That barn was . . . awful."

Her dad pulled out into the road. "I know it's hard

to see the animals neglected like that, but they're all going to be taken care of now, thanks to Trooper breaking out and leading us to them. He's a hero."

Emily grinned. "He is, isn't he?"

Her dad looked over at her. "We think he hurt his leg when he broke free, but the wound on his side had been infected for a long time."

Emily rubbed her jaw. "So he hurt himself to get all the other horses free?"

"He did."

Emily thought about that as her dad drove them back to the farm. "Trooper should have a medal or something."

Her dad smiled. "I think he'd like that."

"I think he would, too. I think I'll make it out of carrots so he can eat it. And maybe apples, too. " Just thinking about doing something for Trooper made her feel better. "So, um, if I hadn't taken Sapphire out and fallen off, we might never have found Trooper, huh?"

Her dad raised his eyebrows at her. "I understood why you took Sapphire, but he's not my horse. You're going to have to talk to your aunt about it. She hasn't forgotten."

Emily sighed. "Yeah, I figured as much." She leaned her head back and looked out the window, watching the fields go by, when suddenly there was a crash and the truck shuddered and she realized Precious was freaking out. "Dad! Precious will hurt herself!"

"I know." Her dad slammed the brakes on, jammed the truck into park, and jumped out of the truck and raced back to Precious as the whole trailer shook even harder.

*H*er dad threw open the door and disappeared into the trailer before Emily could even get her cast untangled from the saddle pads at her feet. The trailer shook again, and Emily finally got out and tottered back, her heart racing.

By the time she stuck her head in the door, her dad was soothing Precious, who had her head in the air, her eyes wide. Her legs were trembling, and her nostrils were flaring. Her dad was soothing her in soft tones, stroking her neck.

"What's wrong?"

"She just got scared being in here alone. Broke her halter." As he talked, Precious slowly lowered her head and stopped trembling. She took a big breath and then snorted on the hay net hanging in front of her.

Emily climbed into the trailer and patted Precious. "It's okay, sweetie. It's just a short ride." Precious's neck was soaked with sweat, and her muscles were tense. "Poor thing, I wish it was close enough to walk her."

"She'd never make it." Her dad pulled a backup leather halter out of the small trunk in front and strapped it around her head. Precious ignored him as she took a bite of hay, munching it with a relish that made Emily smile.

"She's hungry."

"I'll bet she is." Her dad hooked Precious back up to the cross ties and gave her a pat. "She seems happy now. Let's go."

Emily hopped down, and her dad followed, but the instant they stepped out, Precious's head went up and she started to dance in place again.

Her dad jumped back in, and Precious settled down right away and started eating. He rubbed his hand over his forehead, and Emily suddenly realized how tired he looked. "Did you go to bed last night?"

"No." He sighed. "You're going to need to stay back here with her."

"Really? Cool." She climbed in and wrapped her

arm around Precious's neck. "I'll stay right here."

"No, you won't." Her dad grabbed a hay bale that had been shoved against the front wall of the trailer and pushed it up near Precious. "You're going to stand against that wall, and you're going to keep that hay bale between you and the horse. Don't try to grab her if she panics, and keep out of reach of her hooves. If she starts to act up, I'll come back." He gave her a stern look. "Do you understand?"

Emily blinked at the expression on his face. He'd never looked at her like that before, like he was so serious and that she'd be in major trouble if she didn't do what he said. "Yeah, okay."

He narrowed his eyes. "Promise?"

"I promise. Really." And she did. She didn't want to get stomped.

He reached past her and cranked open the window. "Yell if you need me. I'll be able to hear you."

"Got it." She got into place as he stepped out of the trailer, gave her a final warning look, and then shut the door.

Precious snapped her head up, then saw Emily and went back to eating.

"Everything okay?" her dad called from just beyond the door.

"Yep. She's fine."

"Good." There was the crunch of his boots on the road and then the slam of the car door. Emily heard the engine roar to life, and she grabbed onto a hook to brace herself, her heart starting to race as the wheels began to roll every so slightly.

What if Precious went crazy? "You doing all right, Precious?"

But Precious didn't even blink. She simply munched her hay and took an occasional look at Emily to make sure she was still there.

By the time they arrived at Running Horse Ridge, Emily and Precious were best friends, and Emily couldn't stop thinking if it wasn't for Trooper, Precious would still be stuck in that horrible place . . . with a baby on the way. Emily shuddered and gave her a hug while her dad lowered the ramp. "You're safe now," she whispered.

Emily hovered while Precious was unloaded and put into a stall. She was relieved when Uncle Rick announced Precious was in good shape, just undernourished.

Then Emily went and peeked in on Trooper. He was lying in his stall, his forelegs tucked under him as he rested on his chest, his nose drooping to the ground and his eyes half closed. "Hey," she whispered as she opened the door and crawled in to sit beside him. She scratched his ears and gave him a carrot she'd filched from the tack room. "Just so you know, all the horses are safe now. Even Precious. She'll be fine."

He snuffled her hand for more treats, and she smiled. "So now you don't need to worry about them. Just focus on getting yourself better. I'm making you something." She yawned. "I'll bring it in the morning, okay?"

Her eyes were itchy, and her head felt heavy, so she gave him a final pat and pulled herself to her feet, trying not to clunk her cast too loudly, because he looked so tired. She frowned as she looked at him, then she squatted next to him and gave him a hug, rubbing her face against his rough coat, which someone had cleaned up so he was no longer covered in mud. "You did great, Trooper," she whispered. "Really great."

He tossed his head, and she grinned. "Yeah, you already know that, don't you?"

She stood up again, and he watched her leave, making no effort to rise from his bed of thick, clean shavings.

Why would he? He was home now. He could rest.

She carefully shut Trooper's door and then lumbered down the aisle toward Sapphire's stall, her cast clomping loudly on the cement with each step. When she opened it, she saw a fresh bandage on his injured foreleg, and guilt came rushing back even when he gave a whicker and hurried over to her when she walked in. "I'm so sorry I hurt you."

He nuzzled her hand, and she opened it. "I gave all my treats to Trooper. That's okay, right?"

She rubbed Sapphire's neck, marveling at how soft and shiny his coat was in comparison to Trooper's. He was so fit and well fed. Clean. A sparkle appeared in his eye as he gave her a shove and knocked her over before she could catch her balance. She grinned up at him, her heart suddenly feeling lighter. "You don't care about your injury, do you? You think it was fun, running around until you found Trooper, don't you?"

Sapphire put his nose in his water bucket and drank, then moved his head so all the water dripped off his chin onto her face.

She laughed and wiped off her face, amazed at how good it felt to laugh. "It was a long day," she told him. "I needed to see you. You make me feel better."

He nickered softly and started surfing her jeans with his upper lip.

"No ice cream today, sorry." She rubbed her palm over the white blaze on his nose, letting her head drop back against the wall as he nibbled on the hem of her shirt. She closed her eyes with a sigh, breathing in the scent of fresh shavings, of hay, of the fresh water in the bucket next to her head. She listened to the sound of his teeth grinding as he began to munch on his hay, snorting occasionally when he got a noseful of dust.

She smiled and felt herself drift. Just a couple minutes . . . she'd get up soon . . . she just needed a moment with him. . . .

Emily was riding Sapphire in the Norfolk Open instead of Rhapsody, and Rhapsody was watching them with this totally sad look on his face, like he knew he'd been replaced—

"Em?"

She opened her eyes to find her dad squatting in front of her. She was still in Sapphire's stall, and she was curled up on her side in the shavings. She blinked. "Dad? What are you doing here?"

"Looking for you. It's late. I was worried." He scooped her up in his arms and stood. "You had a long day, sweetie. It's time for you to go to bed."

She yawned, too tired to protest being carried, and wrapped her arms around his neck and let her head rest against his chest. "What time is it?"

"Almost ten."

"Ten?" She must have been asleep in Sapphire's stall for hours. She yawned and let her eyes fall shut, too tired to keep them open. "I need to make Trooper's medal."

"You can do it in the morning."

"Yeah . . . " She sagged against him as he carried her out of the barn, her brain already starting to float. "Morning works . . . "

She felt her dad kiss her forehead and smiled faintly when he whispered, "I love you, hon."

"Me, too," she mumbled. "Precious?"

"She's fine."

She nodded faintly, too tired to answer, barely even noticing when her dad set her on the bed and pulled the blankets over her. She just rolled over and snuggled into the sheets and let herself dream of Sapphire . . . and Trooper . . . and Precious . . . and the awful barn with three feet of mud and the horses being hungry and not having enough food and her leg hurting. . . .

She bolted awake, her heart racing and sweat running down her back. The room was pitch-black, her ankle was throbbing, and she could hear the murmur of adult voices coming from somewhere in the house.

Voices raised, and she recognized them as her dad's and Aunt Debby's. They were arguing.

About her!

She nearly fell out of bed in her rush to get to the door to find out what she could hear.

Emily crept down the hall on her hands and knees so her cast didn't clunk on the wood, pausing at the top of the stairs. The adults were in the living room, and their voices carried up the stairs.

She stretched out on her belly to listen, then frowned when she realized they weren't talking about her anymore. They were talking about the farm.

"I don't care about the money," Aunt Debby said. "We have to take care of these horses. It's what we do."

"I know, hon, but there are *forty* extra horses in the barn today, and we're not getting paid for any of them. The stipend we'll get from the state won't cover even a fraction of the care. We don't have the money to pay for them," Uncle Rick said.

"We'll find the money. We always do."

"Not this time." Uncle Rick's voice was gentle. "Deb, we don't even own these horses, so we won't be able to sell them and make our money back. They're just a money drain."

"Then we'll sell Sapphire now," Aunt Debby said.

Emily sucked in her breath and nearly fell off the top stair as she lurched for the railing to get closer so she could hear better.

"No. That doesn't make sense," Uncle Rick said. "We'll get so much more money for him if we wait and get him sharper."

"Well, what choice do we have? Pa didn't leave us much money to run this place—"

Emily's dad interrupted. "Why don't I look at the finances? I've been running my own business for years. I can see where we stand—"

"*We?*" Aunt Debby asked.

Yeah, "We?" Emily thought.

"We," her dad repeated. "I inherited half of this farm, as well, and it's just as important to me."

"But you haven't been here in ten years." Aunt Debby sounded surprised. "You don't care about it."

"I do care. I've been caught up in my life in New

Jersey, but being back here makes me remember how much I love it."

Emily frowned at the wistfulness in her dad's voice. It almost sounded like he didn't want to leave. What would happen in a few days when they were supposed to go back to New Jersey?

"I'll go over the finances, and in the meantime, I can contribute to some of the immediate cash needs of the farm." He cleared his throat. "Unless . . . you don't want me involved. I know it's your deal, and I'll let you run it."

Emily put her hand over her mouth to stifle a squeal of protest. Was that the money her dad was keeping in reserve to buy Rhapsody when they got back home to New Jersey?

"You'll let *me* run it?" Aunt Debby asked. "I doubt that."

Tension began to hum in the room, and Emily pressed her face against the railing, trying to get closer.

"Deb," Uncle Rick said, his voice soothing. "Don't get possessive. Scott's offering us money, and if you want those horses kept here, you'll have to take it. It's a compromise."

The room was quiet for a minute. "You'll really loan us some money for operating expenses?" Aunt Debby sounded so grateful, Emily immediately felt ashamed for getting upset.

But she was still upset. Ashamed and upset. Her stomach hurt, her head was pounding, and she was on the verge of running down there and—

"Of course," her dad said. "We're family."

Family? Emily chewed on her hair while she thought about that. Family. Her dad was the only family she had. Yeah, technically, Aunt Debby and Uncle Rick and everyone were family, too, but they were strangers more than *family*.

"Thanks, Scott," Uncle Rick said. "We appreciate it."

"Don't thank me now. I get bossy when my money's involved," her dad said.

Aunt Debby laughed, but there was relief in her voice now. "He does. We'll never be able to deal with him now."

The adults then started talking boring stuff, and Emily crept back to her bed, trying not to wince as her ankle throbbed with pain. She crawled back onto the soft quilt that Caitlyn had told her their grandma had made like fifty years ago, and she stared at the ceiling.

She counted the number of cracks in the plaster while crossing her fingers that Aunt Debby wouldn't sell Sapphire and that she could still have Rhapsody when she got home . . .

Home.

When she left here, it wouldn't matter if Sapphire was sold. She'd never see him again. Maybe she could get her dad to buy Sapphire *and* Rhapsody. She started getting excited, and then realized her dad would probably make her choose.

Choose between Sapphire and Rhapsody? That would be easy. It would be Rhapsody . . . wouldn't it?

She bit her lip and realized maybe it would be more difficult than she thought.

Emily got up early, realized she couldn't get her jeans back on over her cast, and threw on a pair of loose shorts. She clomped downstairs to the kitchen to make Trooper his medal.

She was finishing up the third layer of sliced apples artfully placed around the outside so it looked like a star when Caitlyn shuffled in, still wearing her pajamas. She yawned, then climbed on a stool next to the counter where Emily was working. "Whatchya doing?"

"Making a present for one of the horses."

"Which one?"

"Trooper."

Caitlyn frowned. "I don't know him."

"He's new."

"Oh." Caitlyn shrugged. "Want to come play in the hay barn today? My fort's really cool, and no one's allowed up there except me and whoever I invite. Which is just Tanya and you." She wrinkled her nose. "Not Kyle. He'd ruin it. And Alison thinks she's too good for hanging out in the hay barn, even though she used to do it all the time."

Emily smiled at the invitation and the hopeful look on Caitlyn's face. "Yeah, okay. I'll try to come later." She remembered well the days of having no one to play with when her dad was at work and she was stuck with a boring babysitter. Life was much better after she starting hanging out at the barn and had horses to take care of all the time and friends to hang out with.

"Really? When? Now?"

"After lunch."

"Cool!" Caitlyn jumped off the chair and rushed back upstairs, shrieking with excitement.

Emily carefully picked up Trooper's medal, realizing that Caitlyn's invitation had made her feel really good. Despite her dad's claim that this was family, the only time she'd felt like anyone at the farm actually cared about her was when Uncle Rick had hugged her hard when he found her in the field, and even that hadn't lasted once he got the call about Trooper needing his help. No one else here even seemed to care much about her, or barely even like her. Except Sapphire.

And now Caitlyn. She might be only seven, but that little offer made Emily feel like she actually belonged here, even if just a tiny bit.

She shoved some extra baby carrots in her pocket for Sapphire and headed out to the barn, promising herself she'd go to the hay barn later on, even if it was only for five minutes.

She reached Trooper's stall only to find the door open and the stall empty. She frowned and looked around, but he was nowhere to be seen. Turned out in a field? He'd like that.

"Emily?"

She whirled around to find Aunt Debby standing behind her, and her gut dropped with apprehension as she realized she was finally going to get her punishment for stealing Sapphire. How bad would it be?

17

*E*mily felt heat rise in her cheeks as she waited for the lecture on taking Sapphire out for a run. "Where's Trooper?" She held out the medal. "I made this for him. It's a medal of honor for saving all those horses."

Something flickered across Aunt Debby's face, something that made Emily's belly tighten.

"Come with me for a minute." Aunt Debby put her arm around Emily's shoulders and led her to a hay bale. She sat Emily down and sat beside her, keeping her arm around her.

It felt good, but also, it felt weird. Why would Aunt Debby hug her right before she yelled at her?

"That was very nice of you to make Trooper a medal."

Emily laid the medal in her lap and straightened out a carrot that had gotten twisted in her pocket. The hay prickled the back of her legs, and she wished she'd worn jeans. "He deserves it."

"He does." Aunt Debby looked down at Emily. Her face was sad. "Hon, Trooper's injury to his side was really infected and his leg was shattered. It was unbelievable he had the strength to get as far as he did from the farm."

Emily nodded. "That's why I made him the medal."

"Yes." Aunt Debby cleared her throat. "See, the thing is, once Trooper got all the horses free, he'd accomplished his goal. He didn't have to keep fighting."

A sense of dread began to rise inside Emily. She stared at her aunt. "What are you saying?"

"Early this morning, Trooper passed away."

Tears swelled in Emily's eyes. "He *died*?" Her voice broke and she clutched Trooper's medal to her chest.

Aunt Debby's arm tightened around her. "Yes, it's a sad thing, sweetie."

Tears were streaming down Emily's face, and her chest burned with grief. "But he can't die . . . "

"He saved all his friends, and he got to go to a place where he wasn't in pain anymore."

Emily stared at the empty stall across from her and started crying harder. "But I made him a medal—"

"Oh, hon." Aunt Debby wrapped her arms around Emily and hugged her, holding her tight. "We can cry for him because we miss' him, but we also need to remember the forty horses he saved. For him, we need to take care of them."

Emily clung to Aunt Debby, burying her face against her aunt's shirt as the sobs wracked her body. "But he was such a hero. He isn't supposed to die—"

"Maybe he was. Maybe that was his job. To save them all so they could live and be happy." Aunt Debby kissed the top of Emily's head and rocked her gently as Emily's sobs began to subside. "He did his job, and now we do ours. It's a team effort."

Emily sniffled, clinging to her aunt as she tried to stop crying, but her breath kept catching in her chest.

"So with all these horses, I'm going to need help around here. Will you help?"

Emily swallowed hard and tried to sit up. Aunt Debby released her but kept her hand on Emily's back, and Emily didn't mind at all. It felt good. Like Aunt Debby really cared. "I guess, yeah."

Aunt Debby gave her a real smile that made Emily

suddenly feel better. Even her aunt's eyes were smiling in a really nice way. "That would be great. What I need for you to do is to go in and clean up each horse. Give each of them a nice warm bath, brush them so all the dead hair comes out, clean out their feet. Make them feel better."

Emily nodded and sniffled again. "I can do that."

"But if one of the horses has a bandage on, check with your dad, Uncle Rick, or me first, okay? And if there's a little red sticker on the horse's name card, then don't go in. That means they are cranky."

"I'd be cranky if I lived in a mud pit and no one fed me."

Aunt Debby hugged her. "I think we all would. Now, hop to it. There are lots of horses that need a good scrubbing."

Emily stood up, clutching Trooper's medal to her chest. "Okay."

"And Emily?"

She winced at the change of tone in her aunt's voice and turned to face her, raising her chin even though her knees had started to shake. "What?"

"Did you see Sapphire got hurt?"

She bit her lip. "Yeah."

"And you did, too."

Her ankle throbbed as soon as she thought about it. "Yeah."

"That's why I didn't want you riding him."

"It was a onetime thing. An accident."

Aunt Debby frowned. "You still believe that?"

"Well, of course. He jumped a stream, and I wasn't ready. He bolted once, and I stayed on fine through that. I wouldn't let him do it again."

Aunt Debby sighed. "I'm sorry you feel that way. I was hoping you'd learned your lesson, and I was going to give you a break, given how everything turned out." She stood up. "But until I see a better sense of responsibility from you, no more riding unless you're in a lesson with me. And I don't want you near Sapphire at all."

"*What?*" Tears stung the back of Emily's eyes, but she refused to let Aunt Debby see them. "But I'm a good rider—"

"That's not the point. The point is that you don't respect the dangers of riding, and you aren't responsible enough to be permitted to ride on your own. When you show me you are, then you can ride freely and I'll be able to trust you with Sapphire."

"But—"

"Trooper's friends need you. You'll be plenty busy with them. You won't let Trooper down, will you?"

"No, but—"

"Good. I'll see you later. I need to go help Uncle Rick with his rounds here so he can get out on the road." Then she turned and walked away, leaving Emily standing in the aisle outside Trooper's empty stall.

Emily felt her lower lip begin to tremble, and she quickly shook it off. Aunt Debby wanted to see responsibility? She'd show her responsibility. She'd take such good care of Trooper's friends that Aunt Debby would have no choice but to admit she was wrong.

Emily deserved to have Sapphire in her life, and she was going to prove it.

$\mathcal{L}$ate that afternoon Emily shoved the metal hoof pick into the chunk of mud packed in Precious's left hind foot. She'd already given Precious a bath, the seventh bath she'd given today. Her ankle was *killing* her, but she was refusing to acknowledge it. She had to keep going. Every time she stopped, she thought of Trooper and Sapphire and started to cry.

So, she didn't stop.

"Got grounded, huh?"

Emily lifted her head, and sighed when she saw Alison leaning on the door, her elbows draped over it, her chin propped on her hands. "Are you going to make fun of me?"

Alison's eyebrows went up. "Why would I do that?"

"Because you don't like me."

Alison's eyebrow went even higher, disappearing under her bangs. "Says who?"

Emily frowned and draped her arm over Precious's back, too tired to hold herself up. "Well, because I do dressage and stuff. You've barely spoken to me since I got here."

"You've barely talked to me!"

"What? No way. It's all you!"

"Me? Not even close. You're the one who hates *me*!"

They stared at each other, then they both dissolved into giggles. "I thought you hated me," Emily admitted.

"I thought you thought you were too good for me," Alison said. "But after you've spent all day out here working on these horses, well, I thought that was kind of cool of you."

Emily grinned. "Really?"

"Yeah. You didn't have to help out like that." Alison shrugged. "It's cool." She eyed Emily. "I also thought that was sort of . . . Well, I was sort of impressed that you took Sapphire out even when you weren't supposed to. I didn't realize you cared that much about him or riding or anything."

Emily felt her cheeks heat up, and she decided not

to tell Alison it was the first rule she'd ever broken. Or first big rule. Her dad had rules, but he didn't really care if she followed them or not. "Yeah, well, it didn't really turn out that great. . . . "

"True." Alison's smile faded. "So, did you hear about Trooper?"

Emily swallowed hard and thought of the medal she'd broken up and doled out to Trooper's friends. "Yeah. That was really sad."

"I know." Alison picked at a stray piece of hay stuck in the door. "He reminded me of my first pony. Same color."

"Really? What was his name?"

"Sammy." Alison smiled. "He was a terror. I fell off him about ten times a day."

"Do you still have him?"

"No, we sold him."

"Oh." Emily scratched Precious's withers. "Do you think your mom's going to sell Sapphire?"

"Definitely. She's been counting on it since she got him." Alison eyed her. "I'm surprised you're even allowed in the barn. She went crazy when she saw the swelling in his leg."

Emily picked up a towel and began rubbing it over Precious's damp coat. She got upset all over again about losing Sapphire and making him get hurt, so she changed the subject. "Caitlyn said you got grounded last month. What did you do?"

"I took one of the horses over the jumps when no one was home."

Emily shot a glance at her. "So?"

"That's what I thought! But my mom freaked because if I'd fallen off and gotten hurt, no one would have been around to save me." Alison rolled her eyes and stuck the piece of hay between her teeth. "I fall off all the time. Who cares, right?"

"Totally. Falling off isn't a big deal."

"Except when you injure yourself." They both looked at her leg. "Does it hurt?" Alison asked.

"It kills."

"So why aren't you inside on the couch?"

Emily raised her brows. "I have stuff to do."

Alison grinned, a smile that said she knew exactly what Emily meant. "Last year I broke my arm and had to wear a cast and a sling. Didn't miss a day of riding."

"I broke my finger two years ago on the day of a show, and I rode all day before I told anyone it was broken. It was so swollen I couldn't even bend it, but I still came in third."

"Well, I got stepped on wearing flip-flops three

years ago and broke four bones in my foot. Rode the next day."

"With stirrups?"

"Without."

"That's the only way."

"Totally."

They exchanged a smile that made Emily feel like she'd finally made a friend. Alison might be a wild rider and be a little crazy, but in some ways they were the same. They understood each other. "I have to run," Alison said. "I have to exercise a few of the horses while my mom worms all the new arrivals. Later!"

Emily felt a twinge of jealousy as she watched Alison stride away, pulling her riding helmet onto her head and strapping it under her chin. Precious snorted as she munched on the hay, and Emily sighed, turning back to work on her coat again. "I'm going to prove to Aunt Debby that I'm trustworthy. I'll find a way." She had to find a way to be allowed to ride Sapphire, let alone visit him in his stall. *She had to.*

But how?

*T*hree days later Emily was furious. She'd worked in the barn for twelve hours a day, taken care of all the new horses, been incredibly responsible, and *still* Aunt Debby refused to let her visit Sapphire. It was time to get help. "Dad!"

Her dad had Jaws on the cross ties in the main aisle, and he was trimming the horse's feet. Amazingly enough, her dad actually knew how to shoe horses as well. It blew her mind what a horsey guy he was and that he'd never told her. Jaws hadn't bitten anyone else since he'd arrived at Running Horse Ridge, and Emily knew it was because he felt the love, but she almost wanted him to bite her dad for holding out on her.

Her dad glanced up, his curved knife in his hand as he carved off some of the overgrown hoof. "What's going on, Em?"

She stood next to him, patting Jaws, wincing at the feel of his ribs under her touch. "So, I overheard the conversation the other night. About how the farm needs money and stuff."

Her dad gave her a stern look. "You shouldn't eavesdrop."

"I know, but I did anyway."

He raised his brows. "Emily—"

"So, anyway, what if you bought Sapphire? Then Aunt Debby and Uncle Rick would have the money they need, but Sapphire wouldn't have to leave. Or we could take him with us back to New Jersey when we go." She held her breath, her heart pounding.

He set the horse's foot down and gave her a speculating look. "Is this because Aunt Debby won't let you near him?"

"It's not fair! I made one mistake and now she's banning me? You know I'm responsible."

"Taking him out wasn't responsible."

"But—"

"But?" he interrupted. "You don't think it was wrong?"

"Only because she banned me. There was nothing wrong with doing it—"

"Then I can't help you."

She set her hands on her hips and felt like screaming. "Why not?"

"Aunt Debby said she banned you from Sapphire because she wasn't convinced she could trust you to show good judgment. If you really believe there was nothing wrong with your decision to take Sapphire out, then I agree with her."

Tears welled in her eyes before she could stop them. "Since when do you not agree with me? You always agree with me."

"Maybe it's time I stopped."

"*What?* Why are you taking her side? I'm your daughter! I'm the one who should matter to you, not all these other people."

He grabbed her shoulders and pulled her close so he could hug her. "Oh, hon, you are the one that matters. You'll always be the one that matters, I promise."

She clenched her fists and kept her body stiff. "So then why are you taking her side?"

He pulled back enough to look at her face. "I'm taking your side. I want you to be safe, because I love you."

"I am safe!"

He gave her a half smile. "Emily, being around here has made me realize how much you've missed out by not having a mom and a family."

She tensed at that statement, and she wasn't sure why. "Why do I need a mom? I have you. You're all I need. Are you going to leave me here when you go back to New Jersey?"

"No, no, no. We're a team, I promise. I just realized that maybe it's not a bad thing for you to get to know the rest of your family. To have someone like Aunt Debby looking out for you, too. Family's important."

She was about to argue, but then she remembered how good it had felt when Aunt Debby had hugged her when she'd been so sad about Trooper. Or when Alison had visited her in the stall the other day. For the first time in her life she felt like part of something bigger. Like maybe she had a place. *Maybe.* "Will you buy Sapphire?"

He met her gaze. "No, I won't."

The regret in his eyes told her the truth. "You used up my horse fund to help out the farm, didn't you? There won't be any horse for me, not even Rhapsody, will there?"

"I'm holding on to the money right now," he said.

Emily gave a shaky sigh. "So what am I supposed to do?"

He ruffled her hair. "I have faith in you. You'll figure something out. Now, scoot. I have five more horses to trim."

Emily was so upset by the conversation with her dad that she couldn't take it anymore. She actually tracked down Aunt Debby and begged her to release the restrictions on not touching Sapphire. Her aunt refused and told her that if she wanted to brush a horse, there were plenty of horses that needed brushing. She hadn't seemed at all impressed when Emily had pointed out exactly how many horses she'd been brushing every day for the last three days.

Emily was nearly in tears when she rushed out of the barn and almost ran smack into Meredith. Meredith was running the hose over Sapphire's injured leg to take some of the heat out of it.

Emily's heart stopped for a moment as she stared at him. His coat was glistening in the sun, he was playfully trying to chew on Meredith's shirt even though she kept pushing him away, and his black forelock flopped between his eyes, making him look like a giant teddy bear.

Jealousy swelled inside her as Meredith giggled and

patted Sapphire. Then Sapphire's head snapped up, and he looked directly at Emily. His ears went forward as he stared at her, and her breath caught at how majestic he looked with his head held so high and his lush tail swishing lightly.

Then he nickered softly.

Emily smiled, warmth spreading over her body. "Hi, beautiful," she whispered.

He stared at her for a moment, then dropped his head and shoved Meredith so hard she went flying onto the gravel with a shout and dropped the lead shank. Then he whirled around and trotted right over to Emily, pressing his head against her belly.

Joy leaped through her, and she wrapped her arms around him and laid her cheek against his forehead. "I missed you, too, Sapphire."

"I've never seen him run over to anyone before." Meredith pulled herself to her feet. "Do you have treats or something?"

Emily smiled as Sapphire lifted his head to peer at Meredith but not take even a single step toward her. "No treats. Just me." She ran her hands over his ears, and smiled at how soft they were.

Meredith set her hands on her hips. "I'm so jealous. I wish he liked me like that."

Emily's grin got bigger. "You think he likes me?"

Sapphire nudged her softly, and she started scratching behind his ears.

"Well, of course. No one's holding on to him, but he's not trying to run away. He ran *to* you and isn't even thinking about going anywhere else."

Emily saw the lead shank was dragging on the ground and realized Meredith was right. She grinned. "He runs away a lot, huh?"

"Whenever he gets the chance, which is why Debby makes us ride him in the ring, instead of the fields, in case we fall off." She gave Emily a sympathetic look. "I heard you got banned from him. What a bummer."

"I know. Do you, um, get to ride Sapphire much?" She rested her cheek against his soft coat, breathing in the horsey scent that was so him.

"A few times." Meredith walked up and aimed the cold water toward his fetlock again.

Emily sucked in her breath. "Did you jump him?"

A huge grin split Meredith's face. "Yeah. It was *awesome*."

"Ooh . . . " Emily held her hand over her heart and moaned. "I'm so jealous."

Meredith's eyes sparkled. "He's an amazing jumper. He snaps his knees so high and cracks his back." The water was completely missing Sapphire's ankle now, but neither of them cared.

"Cracks his back? What's that?"

"He rounds it, so that his nose goes way down between his front feet when he's in the air. It's hard to stay on when he does that, but man . . . " Meredith sighed. "He's so beautiful to watch."

"Isn't he?" Emily sighed, too. "I saw him gallop across the fields."

"With his tail up?"

"Oh my gosh, yes! He looked like he was flying!"

"I know what you mean!" Meredith squealed and clapped her hands, startling Sapphire into a quick sideways jig. "I saw him do that in a field once when he was turned out! Isn't his tail beautiful the way it streams behind him, all black and glossy?"

"Yes!" Emily grabbed Sapphire's lead shank and clutched it to her chest. "It's so thick!"

"I know! And shiny! Have you noticed his dapples?"

Emily felt like her heart was going to stop. "His are the best! Right on his bum, these light brown spots that you can see only when the sun catches them. They're soooo beautiful. And don't you love the way his neck arches?"

"Um, *yeah*. How could you not?" Meredith got a smug look on her face. "I got to help trim him once."

Emily screamed. "No way! Whiskers or ears?"

"Both!" Meredith shouted. "His ears are soooo soft!"

"Meredith!"

They both spun around to see Uncle Rick sticking his head out the window that opened to Precious's stall.

"Yes?" Meredith said. "What's up?"

"I need your help with Precious. Can you come in here right away?"

Meredith paused, then shot a sly grin at Emily. "Is it okay if I let Emily put Sapphire away?"

"It doesn't matter. Just get in here. I need you to hold her." He jerked his head back inside, and Emily and Meredith stared at the window for a second.

Then they exchanged glances and grinned.

Emily squealed and hugged Meredith. "You're the best."

Meredith grinned. "You owe me now."

"Absolutely!" Emily leaned against Sapphire's shoulder, basking in the strength of his rippling muscles as Meredith ran into the barn to help Uncle Rick, leaving Emily and Sapphire alone.

Emily grinned and wrapped her arm around his neck, just taking a moment to enjoy being with him out in the sunshine. It wasn't the same as the freedom of rushing out in the fields, but just being with Sapphire made even the driveway seem special.

The water from the hose began to pool at her feet, so she finally made herself move. She took Sapphire to the faucet and turned off the hose, then she led him into the barn. She thought she heard Aunt Debby's voice and froze, even though she had Uncle Rick's permission.

When Aunt Debby didn't appear, Emily hurried Sapphire to the storeroom, wincing each time her cast clomped on the wood. She hung on to the end of his lead shank while she popped in and retrieved a dry towel and some bandages, laughing when Sapphire grabbed a paper bag of molasses horse treats and starting shaking it, trying to rip it open.

"You are such a pig." She retrieved the bag, pulled out a couple treats for him, and then scooted him down the aisle toward his stall, her heart starting to pound again when she realized her aunt was in the tack room.

She got Sapphire safely in his stall, cross-tied him like Aunt Debby had ordered, then carefully rubbed down his leg until it was dry. The swelling was almost gone, and his leg didn't feel hot to the touch.

Relief made her legs weak and she knelt in the shavings, resting her forehead against his upper leg. *He is going to be okay*. Her ankle was throbbing from the weight of her sitting on it, but she didn't even care.

He nudged her, and she lifted her head. "I love you, you know."

His lips flicked over her pants, checking for ice cream, and she smiled and rubbed his blaze. "I would love to hang out, but I think I better wrap you and get out of here. I'll show Aunt Debby I can be responsible when it comes to you."

She grabbed the thick white fleece, wrapped it carefully around his leg, making sure to wrap inward around the back of his leg so as not to bow his tendon, then secured it with a smaller flannel wrap and some masking tape. Then she repeated it on the other leg for balanced support and sat back on her heels, admiring her work. The wraps were tight, neat, and looked as professional as any she'd ever seen. Even her coach, Les, would be proud, and he was a huge critic when it came to wrapping.

Stretching a kink out of her back, she stood up and unhooked him from the cross ties. She gave him a hug and a promise to come back as soon as she could, then she slipped out of his stall, jumping a mile when she heard Aunt Debby say her name.

*E*mily cringed and turned toward her aunt, who was standing right behind her. "Uncle Rick asked me to put him away for Meredith. He needed her help."

Her aunt gave her an aggravated look. "Emily, it doesn't matter. You knew my rules, and it was your responsibility to adhere to them. You could have found someone else to take Sapphire or helped Uncle Rick yourself."

Emily bit her lip, realizing her aunt was right. She hadn't even thought of it. She had no defense, and stared at her cast, unable to meet her aunt's stern look.

"One more time, Emily, and I'm taking him out of here."

She jerked her gaze to her aunt's face. "What do you mean?"

Her aunt pointed behind, and Emily turned around in time to see Sapphire slide the bolt open with his teeth. "Sapphire!" She ran over to the door and slid the lock shut all the way, making sure it was latched, patting his nose when he lifted his lip in protest of being thwarted.

"Because of things like that," her aunt said. "He would have gotten out again because you weren't careful enough shutting the door. If he gets seriously injured before I can sell him, the farm's in trouble. I already have an offer from Black Dog Farms, a barn in California who buys a lot of my horses."

Emily's stomach dropped. "California?"

"Yes. I showed him to them when they picked up a horse a couple weeks ago. They made me a nice offer that's probably a little more than he's worth today, though I was hoping for more by the time I'm finished training him. I'm seriously thinking about taking the offer, and having to worry about you getting him injured just adds to my concerns. If I can't trust you to keep your hands off him, then it makes sense to sell him before he can get hurt. They're going to be here on Friday to drop off a horse for training, and I'll make a decision by then." She held up her finger. "One more incident with him, Emily, and you'll have made my decision for me."

Then she turned and walked away.

Emily stared after her, her mouth open in shock. "But—"

But her aunt was already gone.

A heavy hand came down on her shoulder, and she looked up to see her dad. "Did you hear that?"

"I did."

He turned Emily and started walking her out of the barn in the other direction. "Aunt Debby's stressed about money right now and she's trying her best to make the right decisions for the barn."

"Why is she holding me responsible?"

"She isn't. She's just trying to find a way to make the right decision." Her dad paused at the ladder to the loft. "Come on up."

Emily frowned, but climbed the ladder, brushing aside hay bits as she climbed into the loft where some of the hay was stored. She took a deep breath while her dad followed her up, inhaling the scent of fresh, green hay. Bales were stacked to the ceiling, and stray clumps of hay dusted the wooden floor. It was hot and stuffy, but in a wonderful way, because the odor of freshly cut hay permeated the entire area.

Her dad motioned her to the big doors used for loading hay from the giant trucks, hauled them open, and then sat down in the doorway, hanging his feet over the edge. He patted the floor next to him, and Emily braced herself on his shoulder while she eased herself down, trying not to fall out the window by tripping on her cast.

When she was finally sitting next to him, her dad motioned outside. "Gorgeous view, isn't it?"

She gazed out and realized it was. There were fields and trees as far as she could see, rolling hills, everything a lush green. She could see the paddocks off in the distance and black and white specks that were horses roaming around munching on the grass. There was even a mountain in the horizon, with a snow-covered top. It was truly magical.

"Aunt Debby's afraid she's going to lose this place. You can see why that would upset her."

Emily nodded, her heart tightening at the thought. She heard the thud of hooves, and she looked down and to her right. Alison was riding Moondance over some jumps, her aunt giving her instruction. The jumps were at least three feet high, and Moondance was leaping over them with ease.

She sighed with envy, wanting to be able to do that, too.

"Debby's right."

She glanced at her dad. "Right about what?"

"Grandpa was more concerned with saving horses than running a business. The farm's in bad shape. They really might lose it, especially now that all these other horses are here. They've had to hire some temporary help to get all the chores done, and that costs money, too."

Emily swung her feet, watching the bits of hay drop off her cast. "What would happen to all the horses if they lost the farm?"

"We don't know."

"Oh." She bit her lower lip. "Jaws and Precious need us right now."

He smiled. "I know they do, hon. Can you understand now why Aunt Debby's coming down so hard on you? She's a great person, and she's trying her best to sort out this mess. I'm helping, but it's not that easy."

Emily shrugged. "I guess. But it's not my fault."

"No, it's not." Her dad started swinging his feet as well, and she stared at the big boots he was wearing, so unlike the polished dress shoes she was used to seeing him in. "She loves you, Em. I just thought you should know that."

She looked at her dad. "Do you think she should sell Sapphire to those people this week?"

"I'm still deciding. I have some decisions to make."

"We can't buy him?"

"No, not today."

She sighed. "So, what, then? How do I keep her from selling him?"

"Try not to increase her stress." He smiled. "I know that's difficult for you, but give it a try."

She nodded. "I guess I can do that."

He put his arm around her shoulders and hugged her. "I knew you could."

She leaned into him, resting her head on his shoulder while she stared out at the vast fields. "Dad?"

"Mmm?"

"Caitlyn says Aunt Debby wants us to stay here forever. Is that true?"

He didn't say anything for a long minute, then he turned his head slightly. "Why? Do you want to stay?"

She chewed her lower lip. "I don't know. I hadn't really thought about it. I was just curious. Do you?"

"Sometimes. I forgot how much I loved being here until I came back."

She peered up at him. "You're a totally different person. Riding horses, shoeing them, wearing jeans and boots. Why didn't you ever tell me?" She touched his face where she could see whiskers. They prickled under her touch. "You don't even shave when you're here. You look like a cowboy or something. I feel like I don't even know you. How could you keep all those secrets from me?"

He rubbed his jaw for a moment while he thought about his answer. Finally, he said, "When your mom and I left town, I wanted to earn lots of money and live an exciting life. I was tired of the farm scene, and a little embarrassed by my background."

"Embarrassed?" It was difficult to imagine her dad embarrassed about anything. He was always confident, so much so that sometimes she'd even wondered if he'd understand her feeling uncomfortable about things like not belonging at the barn. "Really?"

"Really." He looked at her. "And then when your mom died, the farm reminded me of her, and I didn't want to remember. So I left it behind." He sighed. "Now that I'm back, I really regret shutting it out for ten years like I did, and I regret not making you a part of it."

"Oh."

He picked up a piece of hay and stuck it in between his teeth. "But now that I'm back, I realize it was a great place to grow up, and I was sort of thinking it might be good for you, too."

She caught her breath. "You're seriously thinking about staying?"

"Not forever, but for a while. Maybe. I haven't made any decisions. It would be a team decision for both of us. Our plane tickets are transferable, and now that everything is in such an uproar with Trooper's friends, I feel like we should stay a little longer and help out. Is that okay with you?"

"I don't know." She bit her lip. "I have all my friends and Rhapsody. . . . " But here she had Sapphire and Meredith, and she was starting to feel more comfortable with her relatives. And here she had a barn full of horses that needed her. It would be months before Trooper's friends wouldn't need extra help.

He patted her knee. "It's too soon for a major decision. We'll plan on staying a few extra days, and then see how we feel. I can easily keep up with my company from here. Okay?"

"Yeah, okay." She copied her dad and stuck a piece of hay between her teeth.

"And in the meantime, try not to add to Aunt Debby's stress."

She grinned. "I can try. I'm not always that good at stuff like that."

He laughed and hugged her to his side. "Oh, I know. That's one of the things I love about you, Em. Aunt Debby will get used to you, I promise. Let's just break her in gently, okay?"

She saluted him. "I'll do my best."

They sat in the loft, watching the sun until it set. The reds and oranges were breathtaking, the way they turned the trees orange and lit up the sky as the sun sank below the hills. It was truly the most amazing sight she'd ever seen.

And she almost managed not to think about how much more amazing it would be if she was out in the hills riding Sapphire when she was watching it.

Almost.

$\mathcal{E}$mily was late to dinner that night because she had to finish brushing Precious. Her coat was getting softer from all the attention Emily was giving it, and it was turning into a pretty light-chestnut color. She was the sweetest horse, but she looked so miserable being so fat and so skinny at the same time that Emily had spent extra time with her.

By the time Emily slid into her seat at the dinner table, everyone else was half done eating. She'd hobbled as fast as she could all the way from Precious's stall when she'd noticed the time, but she was way late.

Her dad rolled his eyes at her. "You couldn't make it on time once this week?"

Emily grinned as she picked up her fork and plunged it into the meat loaf, knowing her dad wasn't actually mad. "Lost track of time. I was brushing Precious." She glanced around at the table, giving Alison a shy smile. "Hi."

Alison nodded. "Hey, yourself."

Caitlyn tugged at Emily's arm. "You have dirt on your face. Mom doesn't like it when we come to the table dirty."

"Oh. Sorry." Emily rubbed her napkin over her face in embarrassment. "I'll wash up next time."

Kyle ignored Emily entirely, instead pointing his fork at the window behind her. "Max is here."

Emily turned around to see Max, the old gray horse, had stuck his head in the kitchen window and was watching the table with pricked ears, a hopeful expression on his face. She stared in surprise. "Max comes to dinner?"

Aunt Debby got kind of a sad look on her face. "Pa always fed him from his plate."

"I'll do it!" Caitlyn jumped up, grabbed her salad plate off the table, and ran to the window and held it up for him. Max immediately started picking the greens off her plate with his upper lip.

"Don't let him eat the plate," Uncle Rick warned.

"He never eats the plate!" Caitlyn set the plate on top of her head while Max cleaned it off.

Aunt Debby cleared her throat, ignoring Max. "Emily, I know this has been a crazy week, so dinners haven't been consistent, but at the farm we value the together time at dinner. Sometimes it's the only chance we all get to be together, so I would appreciate if you'd make an effort to get here on time."

"Sorry. I'm not used to family dinners." She ducked her head and stared at her plate as she shoved in meat loaf, feeling her cheeks heat up. It had been just her and her dad her whole life, and they ate when they felt like eating. No one set a time for dinner, and her dad would never care if she was late. "I didn't realize it was a big deal."

"Deb, it's not Emily's fault. She's not used to it," her dad said, and Emily shot him a look of appreciation.

"All done!" Caitlyn announced as she marched back to the table and set down her empty plate, looking quite pleased with herself. She picked up her plate with the meat loaf and started to head back to the window.

"Caitlyn." Uncle Rick stopped her. "He doesn't need your meat loaf."

Caitlyn frowned. "He's probably still hungry. I'd already eaten half my salad."

"Not for meat loaf. Sit down and finish your dinner. You can give him more vegetables after you eat."

"But—"

"Horses don't eat meat loaf."

"How do you know? Have you ever asked them if they wanted any?" She turned and faced Max. "Do you like meat loaf?"

Max stretched his head out toward the plate and Caitlyn beamed. "See? He does."

"Caitlyn!" Uncle Rick jumped out of his chair and grabbed the plate out of her hand just as Max was about to chomp down on the meat loaf.

"Scott, you should have told Emily about being on time to dinner," Aunt Debby snapped, jerking Emily's attention back to the table. "You know the rules on the farm. Just because you've been gone for ten years doesn't mean everything has changed."

Uncle Rick put Caitlyn's plate back on the table. "Debby. What's wrong?" He was wearing an old gray T-shirt, and he looked as tired as everyone else at the table did.

Aunt Debby sat back and sighed. "I got a call today that someone bought the horses from Trooper's barn. All of them. We're going to lose them."

"What?" Emily sat up. "But Precious needs me!

What if her new owner doesn't take care of her like I do?"

Her dad cleared his throat. "I bought them."

The table fell into total silence as everyone turned to look at him. "What did you say?" Aunt Debby asked.

He looked around the table. "I took a call today from Linda, the police chief. She said that the owner was going to fight the charges, and she was getting pressure to give the horses back to him." He shrugged. "So I visited the owner and convinced him to sell all the horses to me for a good price. They're ours now."

Emily stared at her dad. "You bought forty horses instead of Sapphire?"

He nodded. "I did."

"Scott." Aunt Debby sighed. "You didn't need to do that. I owe you so much money now." She looked exhausted.

"No, you don't." Her dad picked up his glass of water. "I bought them for myself. I own them. You owe me nothing. It doesn't help with the cost of running the barn, but I couldn't sit back and watch you spend all this money on the horses when you might not be able to sell them and recoup your loss. Now they're an investment."

Aunt Debby narrowed her eyes. "Running Horse

Ridge isn't about making money."

"Which is why you're in danger of losing it." Emily's dad leaned forward. "I own half this place, now I own half the horses here straight out, and I'm spending my money on keeping it going. Therefore, I'm going to see that it starts to make a profit." His face softened. "Would it really be so bad if you didn't have to worry about money anymore?"

Aunt Debby sighed and shook her head. "No, it wouldn't." She finally smiled. "Thanks."

Max snorted loudly, and they all laughed. "He says thanks, too," Caitlyn said, giggling.

Emily was just relieved that Aunt Debby was smiling again. Surely, Sapphire would be safe now, right?

By Friday, Emily was terrified that Aunt Debby was going to sell off Sapphire, and it wasn't even her fault. She'd stayed far away from Sapphire, and helped out with Trooper's friends all day, even when her ankle was throbbing horrifically, which was most of the time. But it wasn't enough because the barn was crumbling under the demands of forty extra horses, even with the temporary help.

Medications were getting messed up, the wrong horses were being turned out, and one day no one even fed lunch and it took three hours until Meredith and Emily had realized it. Aunt Debby was still stressing about money because the horses were costing so much and it would be a while before she could start selling any of them.

But Emily still was having the best week of her life, other than the fact her aunt was on the rampage. It was too awesome to be needed like this, to be crazy busy, to be helping these horses that needed her so much.

"Emily!"

Emily shoved her pitchfork aside and peered into the aisle, around the wheelbarrow she'd stuck in the doorway while she mucked out Moondance's stall. Aunt Debby was standing in the aisle, her hands on her hips, her ponytail half fallen out.

Emily tried to give her an appeasing smile. "What's up?"

"I think someone turned Precious out in the back pasture. I know she's not due for another few weeks, but I don't like having her where I can't see her. Can you run up there and get her?"

Emily glanced at her cast. "You want me to walk out there?"

Aunt Debby followed her gaze. "You're running around here so much I keep forgetting about that." She rubbed her jaw. "Take a UTV out back. I had her out with a UTV the other day, so you should be able to lead her back all right while you're riding it."

Emily stared. "I don't know how to drive a UTV. Wouldn't it be better if I just rode a horse—"

"Learn." Aunt Debby glanced at her watch. "I have to run. Bill and Patsy from Black Dog Farms will be here any minute."

Emily's gut tightened. "From California?"

But Aunt Debby was already rushing down the aisle. Emily's heart started pounding. She'd been so afraid to ask whether her aunt had decided to sell Sapphire, in case her aunt had forgotten. She'd asked her dad a couple times, and he'd said he didn't know what Aunt Debby was going to do, though it sounded like he had his own opinions, even though he wouldn't share them with Emily. She got the sense that her dad and Aunt Debby were both trying to control the farm and were still trying to figure out how to work together on big decisions like selling Sapphire.

"Get Precious!" Aunt Debby's voice echoed around the corner, and Emily jumped into action.

No way was she going to add to Aunt Debby's stress by having her worry about Precious. Not today, of all days. *Please not today.*

Ten minutes later Emily had punched the ignition of the UTV and managed to get it started. Kyle had showed her how to turn it on, brake, turn, and accelerate, and she was golden. After all, if a ten-year-old could ride one, so could she.

Kyle grinned and stepped back as she lurched forward then slammed on the brakes. Then lurched and braked again. He started laughing. "You'll never make it there without crashing."

"I will too." Emily stuck her tongue out at him, then carefully eased forward, her body tensed as she waited for the UTV to explode out of her control. But it moved slowly forward, and she grinned at Kyle as she rolled away from him. "See?"

Then she caught sight of the Black Dog Farms trailer in the driveway, and she drove straight into the side of the barn with a crack that made her wince. Aunt Debby and a couple who must have been Patsy and Bill all looked at her, and she waved. "No problem. I'm covered."

Kyle started cracking up as she shifted into reverse, backed up, then carefully eased into gear, slowly maneuvering down the driveway until she couldn't hear him laughing anymore. Then she clenched her teeth and turned toward the path that led to the pasture. She turned too fast and the UTV started to lean. She squealed, turned back, and almost tipped it over the other way.

She slammed on the brakes, then sat back and put her hands on her thighs. They were shaking, she could feel sweat dripping down her back, and her chest was tight.

"No. I can handle this. Even Kyle can drive one of these things." She wiped her palms on her jeans, took a deep breath, then set her hands on the steering wheel again and slowly eased the UTV forward.

It bumped over the uneven ground, and she winced, afraid it would tip over.

When it didn't, she forced herself to keep driving. "Okay, Emily," she muttered. "You're in complete control. This is for Sapphire."

She kept chanting Sapphire's name and slowly made her way to the back pasture that hadn't seemed so far away when she'd been galloping across the fields on Sapphire. But by the time she got there, she felt like her arms had been rattled off, her brain had been jiggled until it was mush, and her entire body was aching with the stress.

Emily glanced at her watch as she eased to a stop at the bottom of the pasture, realizing it had taken almost a half hour to get back there, even though she'd been going much faster than she would have if she'd been hobbling along on her cast.

She eyed the vast pasture, but it turned halfway up and was hidden behind trees. She saw several horses, but not Precious.

Groaning, she realized she was going to have to drive up there to find her. She climbed off the UTV, her legs trembling as she unhooked the gate, then got back on and drove through. She caught her cast on the gearshift as she climbed off again to shut the gate behind her and had to lurch for the brake when she accidentally kicked it in gear.

She leaned on the hood, bracing her arms as she tried to catch her breath after nearly losing the vehicle. "I hate UTVs," she announced. "They should all be destroyed."

She shook off her nerves and rode up the pasture and around the corner. Then she saw Sapphire standing in the back corner by the fence under the trees. "Sapphire!"

He lifted his head, and she waved at him and brought the UTV to a stop. That had to be a good sign, right? If Aunt Debby was going to send him off to Black Dog Farms, she wouldn't have turned him out in the back pasture, right?

Unless it was a mistake, like Precious. . . .

She glanced around, looking for Precious, but didn't

see her. Had Emily gotten the wrong pasture? If so, Aunt Debby would never believe she hadn't come back to seek out Sapphire on purpose. "Shoot."

She realized suddenly that Sapphire was still standing in the corner, and he hadn't made a move to approach her. Her heart tightened as she gazed at him. "Three days and you forget me?"

He nickered softly and stomped his foot, and Emily suddenly realized he was standing over something large and light brown. "Oh, *no*," she whispered as she slammed the UTV into drive and bounced across the field, barely able to hang on as her hands started to shake. She jumped off it when she got close and hobbled the rest of the way, falling to her knees when she realized what Sapphire was standing over.

Precious was stretched out on her side on the grass, sweating and groaning, the ground churned up under her feet as her ribs heaved with the effort of breathing. "Oh, no!"

Emily whirled to her feet and ran back to the UTV, tripped twice in the tufts of grass and fell hard. Not even feeling the pain in her ankle, she scrambled back to her feet and leaped onto the UTV to go back to the barn to get Uncle Rick. She pressed the accelerator and started to fly down the hill toward the gate, wincing as the UTV picked up speed and bounced over the ruts. She held tight, her stomach lurching with each bump.

As she flew down the hill, she realized there was a sharp dip in the grass. She tried to slow down, but missed and hit the ditch at an angle. The UTV tipped over, and Emily flew into the air, landing on her shoulder and flipping to her back.

She staggered to her feet with a groan, then gasped when she saw the UTV on its side, the wheels spinning aimlessly. Her heart racing, she hobbled over to it and tried to pull it back upright, but it was much too heavy and she couldn't get the traction with her cast. Tears blurred her eyes as she yanked again. "You can't do this! I have to get back to get Uncle Rick!"

When it didn't move, she screamed in frustration and started to half run, half hobble down the hill. Her cast caught in the grass, and she went flying as pain shot up her leg.

She righted herself and started running again, gasping in pain at each step, then fell again. She groaned, holding her leg as the pain ricocheted through her body. "I'll never get back in time."

Then a shadow crossed the sun, and she looked up to see Sapphire standing over her. He dropped his head to give her belly a hard nudge.

"I can't ride you! Aunt Debby will sell you for sure. Remember when I put you away that time? She didn't care about the excuses. *I can't do it.*" She sat up and her ankle throbbed.

He nudged her again.

"No. I won't lose you. *I won't.*" She staggered to her feet, then groaned when she caught sight of the roof of the barn in the distance. It was so far. It would take her forever to make it back.

She glanced back at Precious, who was pawing at the ground again and moaning, and she thought of Trooper. Trooper hadn't stayed home when his friends had needed him. How could she let him down?

She closed her eyes against the sting of tears and wrapped her arms around Sapphire's neck, pressing her face against his soft coat. "I know this means Aunt Debby will sell you to Black Dog Farms, but I have to do it. For Trooper." She held him for a few seconds, then pulled back and took a deep breath. "Okay, let's do this."

She peeled off her sweatshirt, tied the sleeve to Sapphire's halter, then led him over to the upturned UTV. Keeping a hand on him for balance, she climbed up on it, then grabbed his mane and threw herself onto his back, nearly sliding right over the other side.

Her fingers dug into his mane and she pulled herself back to the middle. Then she sat up, gripped the other sleeve of her sweatshirt, and turned him toward the gate. "Let's go save Precious."

She nudged him into a canter, holding on tightly so she didn't slide off, and they headed toward the barn.

Toward Uncle Rick.

And Aunt Debby.

*O*nce they were through the pasture gate, Emily clucked Sapphire into a gallop, gripping his mane tightly and clenching her calves around his smooth belly to stay on his back while he flew across the fields toward the barn. His body was rippling under her, and she could feel every step, every breath, since she was sitting directly on his back. The wind was whipping her face and his body was stretched out majestically as they flew over the fields.

But all she could think about was Precious.

Sapphire skidded around the corner of the barn, and they nearly ran over Aunt Debby, who was standing in the driveway with Patsy and Bill.

"Emily?" Aunt Debby sounded so shocked and furious that Emily flinched. "What are you—"

"Where's Uncle Rick? It's Precious. Something's wrong."

Aunt Debby's face changed instantly from anger to worry and concern. "Where is she?"

"By the back fence in the back pasture." Sapphire's ribs were heaving under her legs, he was breathing so hard, and she suddenly remembered his injured leg. Oh, *no*. "Where's Uncle Rick?"

"Main aisle. I'll get his truck." Aunt Debby was already running for Uncle Rick's pickup truck, which he kept stocked with all his medical supplies and equipment for when he went on appointments.

Emily whirled Sapphire around and trotted him into the barn. She felt terrible when she realized he was limping slightly. "I'm so sorry," she whispered.

Then she saw her uncle walking out the far door of the barn. "Uncle Rick!" She urged Sapphire into a canter, his iron-shod feet echoing rhythmically on the cement floor. "Uncle Rick!"

He turned and looked around, then saw Emily riding toward him. "What's wrong?"

"Precious. Back pasture. Something's wrong. Aunt Debby's getting your truck—"

He was already sprinting away from her and he was gone in an instant. Emily heard the spray of gravel as Aunt Debby pulled up with the truck, the car door slammed, and the engine roared as they sped out toward the back pasture.

Emily sagged with relief, then slid off Sapphire, her legs shaking so much she nearly sat right down when she landed on the ground. He was still breathing hard, and she knew his leg was hurting. "Come on, let's get you cooled down."

She gave him a brisk pat, refusing to think about the repercussions of what she'd done as she led him down the aisle. It was done.

They passed Trooper's old stall, and she gave it a small salute. No matter what happened, it had been the right decision.

Sapphire gave her a hard nudge, and she fell on her butt.

He gazed down at her, his nostrils flaring and his ears pricked forward in a completely innocent look, as if he had no idea how she'd wound up on the floor.

Emily laughed and patted his blaze as he snuffled her jeans for food. "I'll miss you, you know. A ton."

Her throat tightened, and she shook it off as she pulled herself to her feet and grabbed the end of the sweatshirt. "But first, we need to get you a real lead shank. You're way too beautiful to be led around by a sweatshirt."

He followed her happily down the aisle, and she knew that they would be friends for life, no matter where he went.

And she'd miss him forever.

Emily took her time cleaning up Sapphire, knowing it was her last time with him. She was determined to enjoy every last second until he was whisked away. Over three hours later, with Sapphire properly cross-tied and his leg wrapped to keep it from swelling again, Emily was humming to herself and carefully untangling his tail with her hands, one strand at a time, when she felt someone watching her.

She glanced up, then tensed when she realized Aunt Debby was standing in the doorway of the stall, watching her, her face a mask.

Emily caught her breath, then pulled her shoulders back and faced her aunt. "I understand that I broke the rules by riding Sapphire down here, and I know you're going to sell him to Black Dog Farms because of what I did." Her voice broke slightly, and she cleared her throat and continued. "I'm sorry I broke the rules, but

I knew when I did it what would happen. I . . ." Her throat tightened up and she had difficulty finishing. "I know you probably want me to say I realize it was wrong, but I would do it again. I owed it to Trooper and I accept the consequences. I'll miss Sapphire, but it's how it has to be, and I know that." She cleared her throat again, digging her fingernails into her palms to keep from crying.

Aunt Debby crooked her finger. "Come with me."

Emily swallowed and unhooked Sapphire from the cross ties, then carefully shut and locked the door behind her. She limped along after Aunt Debby, trying to will herself to stay calm. Was she going to get yelled at?

Aunt Debby stopped in the corner, next to the biggest stall in the barn, the one that was actually a double stall. She pointed at the door. "Open it and go inside."

Emily frowned and hobbled over to the door and unlocked it. She pulled it open, then gasped at what she saw.

Precious was standing in the corner, looking exhausted but radiant . . . and by her back legs was a chestnut foal with an adorable white moon shape on his brow.

Emily dropped to her knees, holding her hands to her chest. "She had her baby!"

Aunt Debby smiled. "She did."

"He's beautiful!"

The foal lifted his head to look at Emily, his dark eyes brimming with intelligence. His tiny feet were splayed wide as he tried to keep his balance, and his little tail flicked back and forth. His little pink nostrils flared as he tried to figure out what Emily was. "I can't believe how small he is. He's a perfect miniature horse."

"Isn't he?" Aunt Debby squatted beside her, her face glowing as she gazed at the baby. "He's completely healthy."

"He looks like Trooper, doesn't he?"

"I thought so, too. What do you think of naming him Trooper Jr., T.J. for short?"

Emily laughed as T.J. tried to take a step and nearly fell down. "I think it's perfect. Are we going to keep him?"

"You bet. T.J.'s home will be here forever. Your dad said he's giving T.J. to you."

Emily's throat tightened. "Really? To me? Why?"

"Because you saved him today." Aunt Debby set her hand on her shoulder. "Emily."

Emily bit her lower lip and looked at her aunt, trying not to cry. "What?"

"Precious was in trouble when we got out there.

If you hadn't gotten to us so quickly, they both might have died." Aunt Debby smiled, her face the kindest Emily had ever seen. "I saw the UTV in the ditch and realized what happened. That was quick thinking to ride Sapphire back."

"It was the only thing I could think of."

"And you know that because you did it, I'm going to sell him."

Tears stung Emily's eyes, but she nodded.

"And you did it anyway?"

"I had to."

Aunt Debby gave her a thoughtful look. "You did have to. I agree."

She fell silent, and Emily looked back at T.J., smiling when he nuzzled his mommy's belly, looking for a snack. "It was worth it," Emily whispered.

Aunt Debby said nothing, and they sat there in the stall for the longest time, watching T.J.'s first moments of life, laughing at his attempts to walk, smiling when Precious gave him a bath with her huge pink tongue.

Finally Aunt Debby turned back toward Emily. "Okay, Emily, you had your chance."

She looked at her aunt in confusion. "Chance for what?"

"To beg me not to sell Sapphire. To try to justify

what you did. To give me excuses. But you haven't."

Emily stared at her aunt, her heart sinking. Had she blown it by not asking? "But—"

"You knew the repercussions, and you made the choice anyway. You chose saving Precious over your own love for Sapphire, and you didn't try to get out of the consequences." Aunt Debby smiled and ruffled Emily's hair. "You put Precious's needs above your own, and that's what being on a farm is all about. It was the right decision, and it was a mature one. I'm proud of you."

A warm feeling spread over Emily at the look of approval on her aunt's face. "Really?"

"Really. Which is why I'm not going to sell Sapphire."

Emily stared at her aunt in disbelief. "What are you talking about?"

"Today you showed me a maturity that I've been looking for. Sapphire stays. You can't ride him yet, but you can take care of him."

Hope flared deep inside Emily, but she was afraid to believe it. Afraid to open her heart again. "You mean it? You really mean it?"

Aunt Debby laughed. "I really mean it, and I don't joke around when it comes to my horses."

Elation swept through Emily, and she squealed and threw her arms around her aunt's neck. "Thank you, thank you, thank you, thank you!"

Her aunt hugged her back. "You deserve it, Emily. You did great today, and you saved the lives of both Precious and T.J."

Emily released her aunt and grinned at her. "This is the best day ever."

"Because of Sapphire?"

She swept her arm out to indicate Precious and T.J. "Because of all of it. Because this place is the best place in the world."

Aunt Debby beamed at her. "Isn't it? I feel the same way." She raised her brows. "Does that mean you're going to stay around for a while?"

Emily grinned. "I don't know yet, but it's a definite maybe." She hopped to her feet. "Can I go tell Sapphire the good news?"

"Do whatever you want. He's yours to take care of."

Emily hooted with joy and skipped all the way down the aisle, her cast clunking on the cement. "Oh, Sapphire," she called out, "I have good news!"

He popped his head out the door and pricked his ears toward her.

Waiting for *her*.

She stopped in front of him and set her hands on her hips. "Just so you know, I love you."

He snorted, and she knew he was telling her that he loved her, too.

Read an excerpt from the second
book in the Running Horse Ridge series!

*E*mily Summers was on her knees in the main aisle of the Running Horse Ridge barn trimming Sapphire's ankles, and she couldn't stop giggling.

She was peering intently at Sapphire's left front hoof as she carefully glided the electric clippers over the glossy black hair, when she felt something nuzzling her back pocket for the fifth time.

She peeked over her left shoulder at Sapphire's dark brown eyes blinking innocently at her, even as his upper lip was trying to worm the piece of carrot out of her jeans. "I already told you, that's not yours. The fifteen I already gave you are all you're getting!"

He stopped nibbling on her jeans, his dark face

with the white blaze so close that she couldn't resist the urge to give him a little kiss right on the splash of white between his eyes. He immediately lifted his upper lip and grinned at her, then gave her a firm nudge with his nose that knocked her right over onto the rubber mat they were standing on.

Emily laughed as Sapphire pressed his face to her chest, wiggling his black ears as if to point out no one was scratching them. She smiled and scratched behind his ears, and he let out a loud sigh of satisfaction, blowing hay dust across the floor. "You do realize you are so making it hard to get anything accomplished, don't you?"

He snuffled against her, and she realized he was trying to lick her jeans, searching for any remnants of anything tasty, as he'd done ever since he'd found chocolate ice cream on her pants the first time they'd met.

And yes, okay, so maybe she'd intentionally spilled ice cream on her jeans a couple times since then just because she thought it was so cute the way he licked it off. . . .

"Emily!"

Emily scrambled to her feet at the sound of her aunt's voice, brushing the hay off her pants. Had her aunt caught her allowing Sapphire to knock her down? She hoped not. She and her aunt had very different ideas about what Sapphire should be allowed to do, and since

Aunt Debby owned him, she got to make the rules.

And her aunt didn't appreciate it when Emily broke them, as Emily knew all too well. She didn't *try* to break the rules, really; she didn't. It just . . . well, sometimes it just happened.

Wiping her hands on her jeans, she turned to face her aunt. "Hi, Aunt Debby."

Aunt Debby was wearing jeans and worn paddock boots as she always did. Her gray T-shirt had the family farm's name across the front in letters that were so faded Emily could barely read them. Aunt Debby's light brown hair was pulled up in a ponytail that showed her silver hoop earrings. She set her hands on her hips and raised her brows.

Emily winced. Oh, Aunt Debby had so seen Emily allow Sapphire to goof around.

"Where are the cross ties?" Aunt Debby asked.

Emily quickly grabbed a cross tie and hooked it to Sapphire's halter. "If I cross-tie him, then he can't reach my jeans to lick them—"

"Of course he can't. That's the point. We're trying to train him so he can be sold." Aunt Debby hooked up the other cross tie and gave Sapphire a pat.

"But he gets so bored—" Emily swallowed her protest at Aunt Debby's look. "Yeah, okay," she mumbled, hating the mention of Sapphire being sold.

Yes, she'd known Sapphire only for a few weeks, but the thought of being at Running Horse Ridge without him . . . Somehow in the short time she'd been at the farm, he'd become more important to her even than Rhapsody, the horse she was leasing back home in New Jersey.

Emily instantly felt guilty about Rhapsody. She loved him, too. She did. But he wasn't there and Sapphire was and Sapphire needed her and—

There was a soft snort behind her, and she turned her head to see Max, the old gray horse who got the run of the farm, standing in the aisle behind her. "Max!" He'd been following her around a bit lately, and she suspected it was because he missed Grandpa. From what her family had told her, Max and Grandpa had been best friends until Grandpa had died, and Max hadn't been quite himself ever since. She handed Max the one piece of carrot she'd held back from Sapphire. "Here you go, sweetie. I had to fight Sapphire off for it, so appreciate it."

Max gently took the hunk of carrot between his lips while Sapphire perked his ears and watched the old horse as if he was hoping for a stray piece to drop to the floor. When nothing seemed forthcoming, Sapphire set his chin on Emily's shoulder with a resigned grunt.

Max's eyes studied Emily and Sapphire, his jaw moving slowly as he worked his way through the carrot.

Aunt Debby patted Max's neck. "That's nice you're befriending Max. I think he's lonely." There was a softness in her voice that made Emily glance at her aunt. She'd only seen her aunt be that gentle once, when a horse they'd both loved had died.

Aunt Debby was smiling at the old guy, her gaze warm with concern. Emily knew from the look on Aunt Debby's face that Max would never have to worry about being sold. Aunt Debby might be all business when it came to training Sapphire, but there was only love when Aunt Debby looked at Max. Emily felt a tinge of jealousy. Aunt Debby had never looked at Emily like that, even though they were family. Whoa. Since when was she jealous of a horse? That was *ridiculous*.

Emily gave Max's withers a brisk scratch. "Yeah, I think he's lonely, too." Emily wrinkled her nose at the dirt under her fingernails when she lifted her hand from Max's coat. "I'll give him a bath today, and then a good brushing." She cooed at him, "You'd like that, wouldn't you, old guy? Maybe we could get Caitlyn to help." Caitlyn was Emily's seven-year-old cousin. Totally sweet and nice, Caitlyn was the only one at Running Horse Ridge who had made Emily feel welcome from the first moment she'd arrived.

Well, Caitlyn and Sapphire.

Aunt Debby's soft look faded from her face. Her eyes became serious, suddenly all business again. "Later you may be too busy to pamper Max."

Emily cocked her head, not certain how to interpret her aunt's statement. Was she in trouble for something? She'd been working so hard to prove herself to her aunt, to show she was worthy of being trusted with the animals even though she came from a dressage barn and . . . um . . . yeah, okay, even though she'd stolen Sapphire and nearly lost him and had almost broken her own ankle. . . .

She wrapped her arm around Sapphire's head, pleased that he still hadn't lifted his chin from her shoulder. She rested her cheek against his, the fine black hairs so soft against her skin. He snuffled softly, and some of her tension eased as she looked at her aunt. "What's up?"

"How's your ankle?"

Emily flexed the ankle, testing it. There was a slight twinge, but her tightly laced paddock boots immobilized the ankle pretty well, as did the lace-up booty thing that the doctor had given her after he'd taken the cast off a couple days ago. "Feels fine."

"No problems after the lesson yesterday?"

"Nope." Emily had had another jumping lesson on Moondance yesterday, her second one. It had been as fun as the first lesson, and she'd even managed not to fall off, which was a definite step up after her first jumping lesson. It was a little daunting because she wasn't nearly as good at jumping as she was at dressage, and Emily knew that Aunt Debby and everyone else at Running Horse Ridge respected only hunter/jumper riders, not dressage.

Which was why she had to learn how to jump: so that Aunt Debby would trust her and let her ride Sapphire. Emily wasn't worried about her skills, though. She was a good enough dressage rider that mastering jumping would come without too much trouble, as long as she kept doing it. And if she fell off a few more times in the process? Totally worth it.

Emily noticed that her aunt's eyes were twinkling, almost as if she were hiding some big secret.

"I have a proposal for you," Aunt Debby said. "And Sapphire."

"For Sapphire?" Emily frowned, realizing that it hadn't been a casual visit to Sapphire's stall at all. Her aunt had an agenda involving Sapphire.

And with him for sale, that was always a scary thing.

What can *you* do?

Do you want to learn more about animal rescue and how to ride horses? Search online or in your phonebook for local animal rescue organizations and riding lessons.